SOPHIA COBBS was born in 1982 in Dendermonde, Belgium. She has always had a fondness for writing. In high school she wrote poems and short stories but mostly kept them to herself.

This is her first novel.

Besides a vivid imagination she also has some theatrical drama in her life: she is a theatre director, currently practicing in Ghent, Belgium, where she lives.

When she isn't writing or directing, she is doing one of two things: her day job as Office Manager for an IT company, or scouring wine tastings with her long-term boyfriend.

I0564174

Sophia Cobbs'
WONDROUS WORLD OF WITCHCRAFT AND MISERY

SOPHIA COBBS

SilverWood

Published in 2017 by SilverWood Books

SilverWood Books Ltd
14 Small Street, Bristol, BS1 1DE, United Kingdom
www.silverwoodbooks.co.uk

ISBN 978-1-78132-706-7 (paperback)
ISBN 978-1-78132-747-0 (ebook)

British Library Cataloguing in Publication Data
A CIP catalogue record for this book is available from
the British Library

Page design and typesetting by SilverWood Books
Printed on responsibly sourced paper

I dedicate this book to all tea-lovers: may Miss Level's spontaneous tea combinations bring you pleasure

One

Introducing the Most Important Players

A muffled conversation between Petulia and Miss Level was a distraction for all the people in the audience, but they didn't care. They were talking about important things. Like the weather. For some people this might have been a good indication of how badly the actors were performing. I mean, if the weather appeared to be more tantalising than the arts, there could only be something wrong with the arts. Unless the weather was actually extraordinary. I can understand that a hurricane would be very interesting, but the question is: who would go to the theatre in a hurricane?

Clearly Petulia and Miss Level. It makes you wonder if there actually were people around for them to distract. In any case, a performance during a hurricane has a valid reason for being below average. The actors were probably wondering how long the roof would hold up, and they had to shout to be heard over the howling wind.

When one of them finally noticed that the two audience members weren't even paying attention, he signalled to his colleagues and one by one they left the stage to find safety in the basement of the theatre.

The last one shouted, "Switch off the lights before you leave," which made Petulia raise her hand in affirmative response.

And then they were alone.

"Finally! It took them long enough." Petulia grabbed her canvas bag from the seat next to her and stood up.

"Well, you know how daft actors are." Miss Level waited for Petulia to squeeze past her between the rows of chairs, then picked up her own bag and followed. Instead of going to the exit, they crossed the room and walked up to the stage.

Petulia fished a piece of chalk out of her bag and started to draw a pentagram on the floor of the stage. "It's almost ten o'clock. We'll never get this done in time." Three points were already drawn.

"Nonsense. We've got all the time in the world." Miss Level stopped at the first point and put a bowl filled with herbs on the tip. She rummaged through her bag again and found another bowl for the next tip and so on.

When the entire thing was drawn and supplied with the right herbs at the right points, Petulia put her hand in her bag again and found two boxes of matches. She threw one to Miss Level on the other side of the pentagram, who, by some miracle, caught it perfectly. Then she checked her watch: 9:59. She glanced up.

"Are you ready?"

Miss Level had a match in her hand, ready to light it on the box. "Ready."

Petulia kept her eyes on her watch while pulling a match out of her own box. "Now!"

Both women lit their matches, waited a full second with their eyes closed and then blew them out. At the same time as the flames died, the herbs in the bowls caught fire. The women spread their arms and started chanting indiscernible words. The smoke began to whirl around between them, creating a sort of vortex. This went on for ten minutes. Just when Petulia was about to ask if they were doing it right, a shadow appeared in the smoke. First it seemed like the smoke just got darker, heavier. But then it started to dissipate and they could clearly make out the form of a man. The smoke cleared completely and the chanting stopped.

Petulia put her hands on her hips. "Damn it. We did something wrong."

Miss Level, who had a clear view of the man's naked backside and was very distracted by it, asked, "What?"

"He's not supposed to have horns."

Miss Level's eyes slowly roamed up the man's body until she could see the unmistakable horns. She grinned. "Well, at least he doesn't have a tail this time."

Petulia walked around him but couldn't find any other fault in the young Adonis in front of her. "He'll just have to do. Maybe we can use a hat. Those are still fashionable, aren't they?"

"Whatever we do, we'll have to do it somewhere else." Miss Level dropped to her knees and started to put the used bowls back in her bag.

Petulia, who quickly decided she was right, took a sponge out of her bag and started to rub away the chalk. She suddenly looked up. "Did you bring clothes?"

A red glow spread over the other woman's face. "Uhm..."

"Damn it. I told you it was your turn this time." Petulia's hands found her hips again.

"When you're an old spinster like me, people look at you funny when you suddenly go around buying men's clothing." As an afterthought, she added, "Plus, I didn't know his size, now did I?"

Petulia rolled her eyes. She suddenly remembered they were in a theatre. She stood up and walked between the curtains to the backstage area. After looking around carefully, she found a wardrobe filled with costumes. She selected trousers and a shirt that looked more 1960s than Shakespearian and decided they would have to do. When she got back, Miss Level had finished cleaning up the chalk and the young man was still standing in the same spot, naked, looking bewildered.

The problem with creating a man from thin air is that he is just like a giant – albeit very handsome – toddler. Dressing a toddler is not that easy. They squirm and wriggle and basically move around too much. By the time you're finished with them, their trousers are inside out and their shirt is on backwards. Petulia decided not to give a damn, threw a blanket over the badly -dressed Adonis and grabbed his arm to escort him outside.

Miss Level picked up their bags, opened the door for them and looked around the theatre, frowning. She closed the door behind her, mumbling, "I feel like we are forgetting something."

It saw a crack in the ever-present darkness. Its eyes blinked against the light. Slowly it crawled closer to the fissure in the sky. It could see something in the crack. Its hand reached out to touch the crack, but went right through it. Surprised, it moved forward and crawled through the now wide-open hole in the darkness.

It was surrounded by light. For a creature that was used to total darkness, even the slightest hint of light was overwhelming.

With a snap the fissure closed behind it. Startled, the creature turned around, stretched out its arms, trying to find the way back. It took about fifteen minutes before it realised it was stuck, stranded in this world of light.

It looked around, crouched on the floor. It sniffed the floor, knocked on it and was surprised to hear a hollow sound reverberate. Everything in its world was solid. How could something sound like that?

It took a closer look. A brown, solid-looking shape. Rectangular. Nervy. It turned its head and noticed that the floor was made up of several of these shapes, all next to each other.

At this stage the creature had no idea what this was, but it assumed that this thing would have a name, and was set on finding out everything about this world.

Suddenly it grew very quiet, and froze. The colour of the floor crept up its arms and legs until the entire creature was brown, wood-like.

One by one the actors appeared on the stage.

"Well, they are gone." The tallest of the bunch looked around the theatre. "No one left. We might as well go home. The storm seems to have settled."

And with those words they left.

The creature crooked its neck. It lifted its hands and slowly stood up, tall as a man. Gradually its entire body became a fleshy colour and hair sprouted out of its head, the colour of the wood. Its eyes became more human, and the same colour as its hair.

A little unsteadily, it walked forward and left the theatre. Completely naked. It didn't take long for the creature to return and find a red velvet curtain to wrap around itself. Then it left again.

The storm had still been raging when Petulia and Miss Level left the theatre. Of course they were the reason it had started in the first place, so it didn't take too long for the storm to die down. They didn't stop the rain yet, though. That way people would stay inside for a little while longer and Petulia, Miss Level and their package could go home without any problems. Being witches, the rain didn't touch them anyway. Raindrops knew better than to fall on a witch.

Petulia tugged the Adonis forward, while Miss Level still tried to figure out what they had forgotten. The young man was looking around in astonishment and tried to stop at every new thing he saw. Which was everything he saw.

By the time they had rounded the first corner Petulia had had enough.

"It's your turn." She shoved his arm towards Miss Level, who hadn't been expecting any sudden movement, still caught up in her own mind. As a result, Miss Level bumped into Petulia and the young man, hard. All three of them fell down like dominoes.

"Damn it. What is the matter with you?" Petulia demanded.

"Oh, uhm, nothing." Miss Level stood up, wiping her hands on her skirt, mumbling, "I'm sure it's nothing."

Petulia stood as well. Then both women attempted to pull the Adonis to his feet. He was quite content to stay seated for a while, still looking around in wonder, and therefore made no effort to help them. Petulia, who really had had enough of this, cursed and threw a magic word at him; a rather nasty word that shouldn't be repeated. As a result the man immediately stood up and followed them home meekly, no tugging required.

"I should have done this from the beginning." Petulia walked on, stomping her feet. The young man and Miss Level followed in her wake. Suddenly she stopped and turned around. "This is all your fault, you know."

Miss Level, who was still lost in thought, startled. "What? My fault? What is my fault?"

"I am pretty sure you said, 'Cornu' instead of 'Cor'. And now he has horns!" She was pointing her finger towards Miss Level, who took immediate offence.

"Well, I think you said, 'Lituus' instead of 'Litu', so it's all your fault."

The women stared at each other, both with their hands on their hips. The young man was looking from one to the other, realising something more interesting than his surroundings was happening right in front of him.

Miss Level started to give off a faint purple glow. When Petulia noticed this, her eyes widened a little and she backed up a step.

"Listen, it doesn't matter who did or said what. What matters is that we have to get home quickly, before people see us."

The glow vanished and Miss Level replied, in all her distractedness, "Right. Right. We have to get home." She raised her hand to her mouth and started mumbling again. "It must not have been important."

Petulia, who was very relieved that the glow had disappeared, grabbed the young man's hand and tugged him forward, not paying any attention to the mumbling. She and the young man occasionally threw furtive glances in Miss Level's direction, but realising no further glow was forthcoming, they quickly made their way home.

It stood, frozen, outside the theatre, the curtain wrapped tightly around its body. It looked around. Shops with foreign objects, neon lights, letters everywhere. It did not know where to look first.

Across the street, a door opened. An elderly woman showed her face and yelled at it. It turned around to make sure nobody else was there. When the woman shouted again and made inviting gestures with her hands, it crossed the street hesitantly.

When it reached her, she tugged it inside, talking the entire time. She put it in a chair in front of an open fire. The warmth made it drop the curtain and stick its hands out towards the flames. The curtain fell to its waist. When the elderly woman realised that it was completely naked underneath the curtain, the waterfall of words suddenly stopped. Alarmed by the sudden silence, the creature turned and found the woman gaping at it. Then she suddenly left the room.

Not sure if it had done something wrong, the creature looked around. The room was filled with stuff. There wasn't an inch of the floor that wasn't covered up by something, either furniture or rugs. On the furniture were miniature copies of humans. The creature stood and walked towards a table. It picked up a mini-human and turned it around and around. Then it looked at the other dolls. Its head slowly dropped to look at itself. It looked the same, but different.

It heard a gasp, coming from the door, and turned around. The elderly woman stared at it. Then a weird sound emerged from her, an embarrassed giggle, and she stepped forward. Her arms were filled with clothes. She dropped them on the chair in front of the fire and pointed from them to it, babbling all the while. She also kept staring at the wall behind it. It just stared back at her.

When she realised it wasn't moving, she picked up one of the items she had dropped on the chair and came towards it. While she was doing this, she kept looking anywhere away from it and talking nonsense. A giggle occasionally escaped her as she knelt before it and lifted its feet, one at a time, to put them through the trouser legs.

When she tugged up the trousers, she suddenly found herself face to…something else. She turned bright red and quickly got up and tugged the trousers further up. When she had finished zipping them up, she turned and grabbed the clean shirt from the chair. With little instruction – but a lot of talking nonetheless – she managed to put on the shirt.

All the while the creature was paying attention to the sounds coming out of the woman's mouth and realised it was a language. Languages are easy enough to learn, it thought, and concentrated on every nuance in the woman's voice. Not too long after that, it could make out the meaning of certain words.

"Trousers," it said.

The woman startled so hard, she fell back into the chair. She smiled. "Yes, trousers. That's what you're wearing now."

The creature smiled as well. "Trousers," it repeated, smiling brightly, its white teeth shining, happy with this accomplishment.

"And a shirt." The woman pointed to its chest.

It grabbed the white cotton and said, "Sirt."

"No, shirt. Shhh. Shhhirt," the woman repeated patiently.

"Shirt?" The creature frowned. "Trousers? Shirt?"

"Yes. Trousers and shirt." The woman stood up again and walked over to the creature. She put her hands on the shirt and brushed out some creases. "They were my husband's, God rest his soul." A tear formed in the corner of her left eye. She quickly wiped it away. The creature crooked its neck and looked at her, frowning.

"Hus-band?" It lifted its hands and brushed the creases out of the shirt the woman was wearing. She laughed.

"No." She turned her head and looked at the dresser behind her. She picked up a picture frame from the dresser and showed it to the creature. She pointed at the man, standing next to her in the picture. "Husband."

Both of them looked at the picture for a while.

"His name was Adam." Then she looked at the creature, as if seeing it for the first time. "What is your name?"

"Adam."

"What a coincidence." She smiled and put the picture frame

back on the dresser. "How about some dinner?"

"How about some dinner?" The creature repeated it slowly.

The woman turned and motioned for it to follow. "Well, come on, Adam. I have already dressed you, I might as well feed you too." The woman walked out of the door. Adam followed.

A few blocks away, Petulia and Miss Level walked up a couple of steps and entered their house. It wasn't a big house. Well, it didn't look big at first glance, anyway. But if you really looked at it, it seemed to expand right before your very eyes. And if you were ever lucky enough to step through the front door, a whole new world would open up to you. Seriously. When you walked through the door, you suddenly found yourself in a forest. The magical kind, with the greenest leaves, the biggest trees, the crispest air and the brightest sun you could ever imagine. And only a few steps further was a real, honest-to-God gingerbread house.

The young man stared around him in amazement. The door they had just walked through was replaced by a thousand-year-old oak tree, with thick branches reaching towards the sky. The Adonis turned around just in time to see Petulia and Miss Level disappear into the gingerbread house. Not wanting to be stuck alone in this beautiful but vast forest, he hurried to follow them in.

This time, walking through the door only led to a living room. Granted, it was huge, but quite disappointing after the last experience.

Petulia put her bag on the oak table in the middle of the

room. "Well, at least we got back in time."

At that exact moment the grandfather clock in the corner sounded midnight. Miss Level put her own bag on the table and started pulling out all of the equipment they had taken with them. The bowls with the burned herbs were put in the sink. The matches disappeared into a drawer and the chalk was put back in the box marked *Chalk*.

"So what are we going to do with him?" Petulia waved her hand over her shoulder, in the general direction of where the young man was standing.

Miss Level took on a pensive pose and replied, "I don't know," in an equally pensive manner.

Petulia turned around and both women leaned against the table, watching him. The Adonis felt uncomfortable under their scrutiny.

"Except for the horns, there doesn't seem to be anything wrong with him." Miss Level let her gaze wander over his body again.

"Well, we haven't heard his voice yet. We don't even know if he can talk." Petulia frowned.

Miss Level looked at her, also frowning. "Did we include that in the spell?"

"We must have." Regarding him suspiciously, Petulia said, "Say something."

The young man looked at them, thought for a while and then opened his mouth.

"*It's very nice to meet you, I hope you think so too.*"

The two women stared at him, their mouths hanging open.

Petulia was the first to speak. "Did he just…sing?"

"I believe he did." Miss Level was just as stunned.

Suddenly realising that apparently this wasn't the reaction they had expected, he closed his mouth and thought some more. Hesitantly, he sang:

"*I don't know what to say, to make this feel okay.*"

Again, this didn't seem to be what they wanted so he shut up and stared back at them.

"Well, at least he knows the English language." Miss Level turned to Petulia, gauging her thoughts. Petulia had none.

"Huh." That was all she was capable of saying. Then she turned and walked up the stairs.

Not quite knowing what else to do, Miss Level got some blankets and a pillow and showed the young man where he could sleep. On the sofa, of course; they were respectable spinsters – even though they did go around creating young handsome men every once in a while.

The Adonis laid himself down, his eyes fluttered closed and he was asleep in a heartbeat. Miss Level watched him for a while, tucked him in – nice and tight – and then retreated to her own bedroom.

The next morning Adam went through the elderly woman's wardrobe. He flipped through her husband's clothes.

"No." Flip. "No." Flip. "No." Flip.

Suddenly he grabbed his stomach and winced. The evening before had been very educational – he had learned an entire language in one night – but the dinner was upsetting his stomach. He had to remember that old people were too bony and not fleshy enough. Well, you live and learn.

He burped, smiled and went on going through the clothes.

"No." Flip. "No." Flip. "No." Flip.

Miss Level had her eyes closed when she came out of her room and walked down the stairs. She was letting her nose lead the way. She inhaled deeply, the smell of blueberry pancakes filling her nose and making her mouth water.

"Good morning, Petulia," she said.

The reply she got was not entirely what she had been expecting.

"Good morning to you, I hope you slept well. Would you like some pancakes too? You might just as well."

Miss Level's eyes flashed open and she stared at the young man, who was expertly pouring batter into a skillet. She nodded her consent when he glanced up at her. Thinking she might as well enjoy the view – he was wearing only his inside-out trousers – she sat down at the table, put her chin in her hands and gazed at him dreamily.

At the same time Petulia, who had been up for a while and was in an extremely foul mood, was picking apples outside. She had had a horrible dream about a strange man having a rather remarkable dinner and couldn't shake the feeling that it was just the beginning. To top it off she had come downstairs and found the Adonis standing at the kitchen sink, rinsing blueberries. It took a while before she realised what this meant: this would be the first time in a hundred years that she would not be making breakfast. She couldn't leave it at that, so she had picked up a basket and walked out. And now she was here, picking apples and rambling on and on, to a bluebird of all things. She could not believe she had sunk this low, so she turned around and walked back home.

When she walked through the door the smell of blueberry pancakes hit her. She put the basket on the table and sat down next to Miss Level. At least she could make an apple cake later. That would brighten her day. Now she just needed something to keep her mind from reliving her dream.

"He needs a name. He's our seventh try, right? That would be 'G'." Petulia thought for a while. "How about Gerald?"

Miss Level snorted. "He doesn't look like a Gerald." Her lip twitched and quirked into a half-smile. "He looks like a God. Well, except for the horns."

Petulia's head snapped towards Miss Level. "We cannot call him God. The real one would be furious."

"How about Giovanni? We could call him Gio for short."

"He doesn't really look Italian." The heads of both women tilted to the right as they continued to size him up: the mid-length blond hair with a slight wave in it, his bright blue eyes, his aristocratic nose and square jawline.

"That's a face made for sculpting coins in its image," Miss Level said dreamily.

"If I remember correctly, that was part of the plan. Without the horns, of course." Petulia paused for a minute. "You do realise we have to show him to her, don't you?"

Miss Level winced. "She won't want him with those horns." She tilted her head again. "You know, they are kind of growing on me. I think they are adorable."

"Regardless, I'll set up a meeting for today." Petulia let her gaze wander up the young man's body until it landed on the unmistakable horns. "At least we can show her we're making progress." Doubtful.

Adam had found a grey pinstriped three-piece suit with matching bowler hat and cane. Amazingly enough, it fitted him perfectly.

He opened the front door and walked out into the street. It was misty outside and the sun had trouble guiding her sunbeams to the earth. Adam looked around, smiled, and decided on good luck to go left.

"What about George?" Petulia asked through a mouthful of blueberry pancake.

"Or Giorgio. And then we could call him Gio for short." Miss Level's eyes sparkled.

"Or Geoffrey."

"Or Giogio. And Gio for short."

"I'm picking up a pattern here," Petulia remarked drily. She watched the young Adonis clearing his own plate of blueberry pancakes. "I like Gabriel. What do you think?"

"Oh, all right. As long as I can pick his nickname."

"Let me guess. Gio?"

Smiling broadly, Miss Level replied, "How did you know?"

"Fine. Gabriel Gio as his full name. Deal?"

"Deal." The women shook hands on it and then commenced with teaching the young man his name. And their own, while they were at it.

Two

Why All the Men?

About half an hour later there came a knock on the door. Miss Level dried her hands on her apron – she was just in the middle of doing the dishes – and went to open it.

A gorgeous young woman was standing there, completely dressed in white. Her amber curls dropped below her waist. A small tiara, made up of Swarovski crystals, rested atop her head. The sleeves of her evening gown were just as puffy as the rest of the dress and the entire thing was covered in small pearls and silver beads.

"Hello, Princess Clarice, won't you come in?" Miss Level did her best to be as polite as she possibly could; which was very hard because she disliked Princess Clarice with her entire being.

"Of course I will." The high, staccato voice of Princess Clarice cut through the house. When she moved forward the hoop of her skirt got stuck on the other side of the doorjamb; the dress did not fit through. She stepped back and tried again, with the same result. Miss Level came up to her and lifted the hoop sideways. This way Princess Clarice's backside was visible to the entire forest, but she was able to come into the house.

Petulia, alarmed by the voice of Princess Clarice and all of the ruckus that accompanied her entrance, stood up from her writing desk in her study at the back of the house. She took a deep breath and realised that she would need a lifetime of breaths to calm down enough to face Princess Clarice, and that she just didn't have the time. She put her writing equipment together in a neat pile and turned around. Gabriel was staring at her from the chair near the door.

"It will be all right, Gabriel." She winked at him. "I'll be back as soon as possible. Just stay here for a while and read some more." Then she opened the door, took another deep breath – it was a habit when faced with Princess Clarice – and walked into the main room.

"Princess Clarice, so nice to see you. I was just writing you a letter to invite you over." Petulia held out her hand to shake the other woman's, and then realised this would never happen and curtsied instead. Miss Level snickered.

"Yes, well, a little birdie told me you two were back so I decided to come by."

Stinking bluebird, thought Petulia, that's the last time I ever say hello to him when I'm picking apples. But she smiled and said, "Well, I'm glad you are here. Will you join us for some tea?" She walked over to the kitchen, but was stopped dead by Princess Clarice's next words.

"No, I want to see my order first. Where is he? He better not have a tail this time."

"He doesn't. I swear." Petulia turned to face Princess Clarice.

"Or scales? You do admit that that was not your best work, don't you?" Princess Clarice walked over to the sofa. She regarded it suspiciously but finally decided to take the chance with her hoop skirt. The effect was hysterical and it took all of Miss Level's self-control not to burst out in laughter and roll around on the floor. Petulia, who wasn't naturally inclined to appreciate humour in anything, just kept her face straight as usual. She did throw a nervous glance towards Miss Level, hoping she wouldn't ruin everything.

It had taken a lot of persuading to finally get Princess Clarice to place her order with them and not with the Briar sisters. Granted, they were twins and possessed that natural ability for magic, which made them better, but Petulia had given Princess Clarice an offer she just hadn't been able to refuse: a gigantic discount.

With the hoop completely surrounding her and the fringe of her dress forming a puffy cloud of tulle, Princess Clarice did her best to appear regal. "Well, where is he then?"

"To be honest, we are still prepping him for your meeting." Petulia figured she had to stall. "Do you really want to meet him like this?" she asked hesitantly.

Princess Clarice lifted her chin and demanded, "Like what?" Of course she knew exactly what Petulia was talking about. She looked ridiculous, with the hoop almost around her head, drowning her in a sea of tulle, but she would rather die than admit that she had done something wrong or inappropriate.

"He is still a little rough around the edges," Petulia said, completely ignoring the ridiculousness of the tableau in front of her.

"Some edges rougher than others," Miss Level mumbled, disguising it – not very well – with a cough.

Princess Clarice was oblivious to this, of course. She also didn't want to spend any time on something that might not be favourable to herself.

Petulia went on as if nothing had happened. "We were going to teach him how to stand properly, how to escort you around, how to dance. In short, we were going to teach him all the things he would need to know and do to be your perfect man. Of course, if you want to meet him now, you can. I just fear that you might be inclined to cling to the image of the man you would see now, instead of the fully formed man you will get later. But if that is what you want…" With those last words Petulia slowly walked across the room to the door of her study.

"Well," Princess Clarice started, "can you guarantee me that he doesn't have a tail, a third eye, scales, cloven hooves for feet, a beak or a trunk?"

"Yes, I can guarantee that." Petulia kept a straight face and hoped furiously that Princess Clarice wouldn't look at Miss Level, whose mouth was hanging wide open but who clearly couldn't form any words of her own.

"Well, all right then. I expect him to be fully trained by the next full moon. That is when I will have my birthday party and I will take him out in public." Princess Clarice started rocking back and forth, trying to lift herself out of her sitting position. Because of this she could not see the entire conversation being conducted entirely through facial expressions between Petulia and Miss Level. By the time Princess Clarice had managed to rock herself free from the sofa – this took about fifteen minutes – the two women had silently agreed to have the entire conversation again, but verbally, when the princess had left.

Princess Clarice was now fully upright and turned towards Petulia and Miss Level. Her face was pink with exhaustion and she was breathing heavily.

"Well, all right then." She put her hands on her waist and bent over a bit. "I'm going to leave now…right now…I am getting ready to go…just you watch…going…" Suddenly she stood up straight and nodded at Petulia, then at Miss Level. Another minute of waiting before she turned around and finally made it to the door. She pulled it open, lifted her hoop sideways and wriggled her way through. Petulia closed the door behind her.

"So, what was that about?" Miss Level put on a squeaky, high, whiny voice and mimicked Petulia: *"Yes, I can guarantee that."*

Petulia rolled her eyes and replied crossly, "Damn it. He does not have a tail, a third eye, scales, cloven hooves for feet, a beak or a trunk, now does he?" She looked expectantly at Miss Level. No reply came forth. "So I could guarantee that, couldn't I?" She lifted her shoulders uncaringly. "He just has horns."

"Yes, he just has horns," Miss Level mocked. "She probably won't even notice them." Sarcasm did not become Miss Level, and she was not very good at it. People generally did not know when she was being sarcastic, which was the case now with Petulia.

"Do you think so?" Petulia's index finger and thumb found her chin and she rubbed it vigorously in thought. "Maybe we should revisit the hat idea."

Miss Level could only respond with a stare. When Petulia faced her she finally realised that what she had said had been sarcastic.

"All right then. What is your brilliant idea?" She put her hands on her waist and started tapping her left foot.

Miss Level thought long and hard – this had been known to take several days – and asked hesitantly, "Could we use magic to make the horns disappear?" She chanced a glance at Petulia. When no worthwhile reaction appeared, she continued. "We do not have the time to try and make a new man. It would take too long to prepare the spell. And don't forget that the full moon is only three days away. We cannot go back and forth in that short time period. So can we, I don't know, try and dissolve the horns?"

The brows of both women furrowed. They looked at each other without seeing one another, both lost in thought. You could have put a mirror between the women and seen the same image – only slightly different because, let's be honest, they really looked nothing alike. Petulia was tall and slender with a firm expression constantly fixed upon her long face. Miss Level was about two feet shorter and curvy with a heart-shaped face and lovely blue eyes. But the motions were all the same, if you know what I mean.

Petulia was the first to break the pose. "We will consult *The Big Book of Dale*."

Miss Level nodded and followed her to the study.

The soft tick of Adam's cane resounded on the street. Not many people were outside. It was still wet out and a few trees had been picked up and thrown a few feet further, as if they were mere toothpicks.

Adam let his eyes scour his surroundings. The red-brick houses with nice tiny gardens in front of them seemed to go on and on. It was one after the other.

The smile that had been on Adam's face since he had left the house had vanished after one block. Always the same – how boring. Didn't these people have their own thoughts and ideas? Whose example were they following? What boring person was their leader?

He went a few steps further and suddenly stopped dead in his tracks. Blue shutters and a yellow door. The front garden was filled with daisies, and the picket fence was painted purple.

Adam was astounded. What a unique house. What an epiphany in this dreary street! He tapped the cobblestone street underneath his feet with his cane, tipped his bowler hat and marched across the street to the very house that had caught his attention.

Three

The Big Book of Dale

Gabriel was still sitting in the same chair near the door in the study. He had been sitting in the same spot the entire time Princess Clarice had been there and had heard everything that had been said about him. He lifted his hand to his horns and sadly caressed them.

The door opened and Petulia and Miss Level entered the study. Gabriel pretended to brush his hand through his hair, cleared his throat and went back to the book he was reading. Petulia and Miss Level didn't really pay any attention to him. They walked right up to the giant bookcase that covered the entire opposite wall and started searching for *The Big Book of Dale*.

"Alchemy, biology, geology – this is the science section with everything ending in –y." Miss Level's finger caressed every book it passed while she called out the titles.

"*Rapunzel, Little Red Riding Hood, Sleeping Beauty*. This is the history section." Petulia raised her head to look at the shelf above it. "Ah, the encyclopaedias. It might be somewhere on that shelf." She looked around and finally noticed Gabriel by the door. "Oh, there you are."

Gabriel smiled.

"Would you mind standing up? I need the chair you are sitting on." Petulia walked towards him. Gabriel stood. She swiftly grabbed his chair and dragged it across the floor to the bookcase. She climbed on top of it and let her gaze travel across the spines of all the encyclopaedias.

Gabriel looked lost. He had no idea what was going to happen but somehow knew that, whatever it was, he wasn't going to like it. His hand moved up to his horns again, unconsciously. His fingers gently rubbed their soft ridges and he lost himself in pondering.

This was the moment Miss Level turned around and saw him. She was struck by how sad he looked. She cast a quick glance at Petulia, who was still going over the encyclopaedias, and suddenly decided to help Gabriel. He was a man – even though they had created him from scratch – and he had feelings like any other person. He was also only one day old, technically speaking. So he couldn't really help himself, now could he?

Miss Level looked back at the bookcase and her gaze immediately fell upon *The Big Book of Dale*. It was a flashy red. How on earth they had missed it before was a mystery. Perhaps the book didn't want to be found until it was the right time. Let us stick with that theory.

When Miss Level noticed *The Big Book of Dale*, she startled. Her eyes flitted sideways to Petulia. Then she quietly mumbled a few words. *The Big Book of Dale* shrank and shrank. The bright red colour turned a mossy kind of green. On the spine of the now *Tiny Book of Dale* it just said *BBD* – there wasn't any room for anything else. Miss Level looked over her shoulder, a little guiltily. Gabriel stared at *The Tiny Book of Dale*. Then his eyes went from the book to Miss Level and back – kind of like during a tennis match. Miss Level smiled and winked at him. He hesitantly smiled back.

"Damn it. It's not here." Petulia was standing in her most natural pose – hands on her waist – but this time she was on higher ground; or should I say furniture? "Did you find anything?" Petulia turned and looked at Miss Level.

"Nope. Nothing. Not a thing." Realising she was attracting too much attention with all the denials she was spewing, Miss Level snapped her mouth shut.

Petulia arched one brow and just looked at her. This made Miss Level feel very uncomfortable. She lifted her gaze to the top of the bookcase, as if in search of *The Big Book of Dale*.

"Well, all this searching is making me kind of thirsty. How about a cup of tea?" With those words Miss Level turned and walked out of the room to the kitchen. Petulia just shrugged, climbed down from the chair and followed.

Gabriel, who had been watching everything and didn't know what to think about it all – keep in mind, he was only one day old – shrugged as well and followed, closing the door behind him.

The tiny version of *The Big Book of Dale* started to move. An observer might be inclined to describe it as hopping. The transformed *Big Book of Dale* hopped up and down – tiny hops of course – until it reached the edge of the shelf. There it waited for a minute, as if to gather its courage, and then it leaped off the shelf. It landed with a small thud, opened, spine on the floor, pages fluttering in the breeze caused by the jump. The covers – front and back – started to lift and drop. The book flapped, like it wanted to fly. The movement caused the tiny *Big Book of Dale* to rock. Suddenly the momentum got the book upright. Then it sort of walked across the floor. It used its hard cover to wiggle over to the door. There it stood against the wall and just waited.

Adam stood in front of the yellow door. He had knocked but nobody had answered. He stepped back to see if he could see a light inside. He focused on the house and it seemed to expand right in front of him. Amazed and confused, he shook his head. But when he focused again, the house started to contort once more into a huge mansion.

Adam tilted his head and decided to try and see if the door was open by any chance. He walked up the steps and put his hand on the doorknob. It turned, so he pushed open the door and found himself staring at the greenest environment he had ever seen – which actually isn't saying that much. Adam looked over his shoulder at the dreary grey street with the repetitive pattern of houses. He straightened his jacket, put his bowler hat on straight and hooked his cane into the crook of his left arm. Then he pushed the door open wider and stepped through.

Miss Level, Petulia and Gabriel were sitting at the kitchen table. The kettle was on the stove. Miss Level took three cups out of the cupboard and put an assortment of teas on the table. She leafed through the different kinds: camomile, camomile with mint, camomile with cranberry, camomile with honey, white tea with pear, green tea, green tea with lemon, Earl Grey, Turkish apple, mint, rosehip, rosehip with raspberry, all kinds of fruit teas (strawberry, peach, blackcurrant, several types of berry...), and just regular tea.

Petulia grabbed one of the regular teabags and shook it to get rid of the tiny particles of tea leaf that might be attached to the outside of the bag. Miss Level decided to mix and match. She took a bag of camomile and one of mint. Then she went back to the cupboard and pulled out all sorts of pots with herbs. They were usually used for magic spells, but Miss Level felt lucky. She took a cinnamon stick, some rose petals and a few dried hibiscus leaves. She put all of them in a paper filter and went back to her seat. She grabbed the two teabags she had already taken and put everything in her teacup. Just then the kettle started whistling – although screeching would probably be a better description.

Gabriel had been watching Petulia flap her teabag and Miss Level's entire tea construction. He shrugged, took the box with the tea assortment, lifted it to his nose and smelled every different kind of tea. He smiled when he smelled the white tea with pear, put the box back down and took out one of those bags. Still smiling, he watched the women watching him and he did what Petulia had done – shook it like a Polaroid picture – although he had no idea why she had done that.

Miss Level stood up again, put the gas down and lifted the kettle, with the aid of a towel, off the stove. She came back to the table and filled everyone's teacups. She put the kettle back on the stove and sat down. All three of them picked up their teaspoons at the same time and stirred their tea. As an afterthought Miss Level twisted around in her seat, opened the drawer behind her and pulled out a tin box. When she put it on the table and opened it, Gabriel could see that it was filled with cookies – chocolate chip. He quickly realised that this was another smell he liked – a lot. He regarded Miss Level, who had been watching his reactions. She picked up a cookie for herself and then nodded to Gabriel to go ahead. He immediately reached for a cookie and did the same as he had done with the tea – lifted it to his nose and inhaled deeply. He bit into it and closed his eyes as if in ecstasy.

During all of this Petulia had been stirring her tea, deep in thought. "The book cannot just have vanished. It has to be in the study," she mumbled.

Miss Level, of course, pretended not to hear anything, and Gabriel was wise enough to follow her example.

The door he had walked through had vanished the minute Adam set both feet on the grass. A giant tree was now where the door had been. No houses, no street.

"How peculiar." Adam put his right hand against the tree trunk. "Solid as a rock. Very peculiar." He looked around the trunk but could see nothing but forest.

It was amazing, though. It looked as though it might have been painted by a very optimistic artist. The green of the grass and the leaves was what green was meant to be like. The flowers, sprinkled all over the forest, between the trees, were of the brightest colours.

Adam bent down and picked one of the finer specimens: a forget-me-not. However, the moment the stem snapped off, the flower wilted and died between his fingers. Adam startled and looked down at the ground. Where the flower had been, a small, brown, shrivelled-up piece of stem was all that was left. As he looked a bit closer, he noticed that the grass beside the flower was shrivelling up as well. He waited for a while to see if it would spread further. At a circumference of about an inch the shrivelling stopped.

Adam looked back at his hand. The part of the flower he had picked had turned to ash. He rubbed his fingers together, which only made the spot of ash bigger. Agitated, he rubbed his hand against his trouser leg.

Adam looked up and noticed a path a little further along. It wasn't a made path; it was a worn path – worn by years of walking in the same direction over and over again. Trusting in Lady Luck, Adam turned left onto the path and followed it to wherever it would lead.

If he had turned right, he would have immediately seen Petulia and Miss Level's gingerbread house. He would have walked up to it and knocked on the door, curiosity driving him to do so. Miss Level would have risen from her seat at the kitchen table and opened the door. She would have immediately realised what they had forgotten in the theatre, just by looking at Adam. And then, of course, the story would pretty much end.

Luckily, Adam turned left and walked towards uncertain adventure.

*

Miss Level was staring at her now-empty cup of tea. The combination of ingredients she had gathered had turned out to be quite exquisite and Miss Level knew – just like everyone else does – that she would never be able to make that same cup of tea again. She should have written down the amounts she used of every ingredient. But, being an adventurous witch – at least when it came to tea – this wasn't the first time she had created a new tea combination. Previously she had always written down her recipes, but after so many failures, she had decided to stop doing that. Now she was wondering if perhaps that was the reason why the tea had turned out so well.

Petulia was still wondering where *The Big Book of Dale* had disappeared to.

And Gabriel was wondering if there were any cookies left.

After about a fifteen-minute walk the amazing forest gave way to a beautiful meadow. There were a few sheep grazing in the grass and a scruffy-looking sheepdog was lying not too far from them, watching them.

Suddenly the dog sat up. His ears shot up straight. He sniffed the air, immediately sprang to his paws and started barking in Adam's direction. He jumped around, nervously and angrily at the same time, trying to catch someone's attention and alert him or her that the flock of sheep was in serious danger.

But nobody besides Adam was around, and he only noticed how tasty the sheep looked.

Four

The Predictions

Miss Level's ear started to itch. She was still deep in thought about the tea, so it took her several minutes of absently scratching her ear before she realised what it meant. Her head snapped up towards Petulia, who was still pondering the disappearance of *The Big Book of Dale*. Gabriel had already abandoned his musings about cookies and immediately regarded Miss Level with apprehension.

"Petulia," Miss Level said, "my ear is itching."

"Hmm," was all Petulia said in response to this very disturbing news.

"I said, my ear is itching." Miss Level looked nervously at Petulia.

"Yes, I heard," Petulia replied absently.

Miss Level put her hand on Petulia's arm. At this sudden contact Petulia stopped staring into her empty cup of tea. The look she gave Miss Level was unmistakable.

"Why did you disturb me? This better be good."

With clear articulation and in a loud voice Miss Level repeated, "My ear is itching."

Petulia just stared at her for a minute like she was an idiot. Just when Miss Level was on the verge of attempting sign language, comprehension dawned on Petulia. Her eyes opened wide and her mouth dropped open too.

She whispered, "Are you sure?"

"Of course I'm sure," Miss Level replied testily. "It is red and swollen from all the scratching that I have been doing."

Petulia put her head in her hands and whispered, "Oh God, this is it."

A long time ago God had come for a visit. He was a stocky little man with a white beard and long white hair. He had been angry with them for something they had done, but none of them remembered what it was – although there was a rumour going around that it had something to do with an apple tree and a snake.

They had been surprised to see him but had invited him in for tea anyway. All three of them had gone through all of the small talk they could think of before the water had even started to boil. Not knowing what else to talk about, they had decided it would be fun to play a game of Predictions.

The rules of this game were simple: each of them had to make two predictions, and the predictions had to concern the other two competitors. Then, whoever was right twice first, won. As you can probably guess, the game had not ended yet. But more importantly, God's first prediction had already come true, so Petulia and Miss Level were a little concerned about the second one.

Just so you can follow everything I will fill you in on all of the predictions. God's predictions were: one – that Petulia would find a book with all of the answers in it, and two – that Miss Level's ear would itch and that this would be the beginning of the end.

When Petulia had found *The Big Book of Dale*, she had been obliged to tell God that his first prediction had come true. They had cast a spell on themselves at the end of the game, which made it impossible not to share any outcome – good or bad – with the other competitors.

At the news of his first victory God had gleefully laughed and repeated, "I told you so," over and over again until Petulia had slapped him in the face. This, of course, had made him angry again and he had shouted something obscene and stomped off.

Petulia and Miss Level's predictions had not yet come true. It was even worse: their predictions hadn't even been in the vicinity of coming true. Of course – and this was a glitch in the rules of the game – they had never agreed on a time limit, so it was very possible that their predictions would come true in another two hundred years. But let's not think about that for now. I will, however, tell you their predictions so you can judge for yourselves.

Petulia's predictions were: one – that God would meet his match, and two – that Miss Level would create the perfect spell. Miss Level's predictions were: one – that God would unwittingly destroy Heaven, the city where he lived, and two – that Petulia would meet the man of her dreams.

"Damn it, we should never have played that stupid game." Petulia still had her head in her hands.

"Well, it's too late now." Miss Level sighed. "What are we going to do?"

Silence.

"We could go back in time and hand ourselves a note that says we cannot play the game," Miss Level suggested. "Or that we cannot open the door to anyone that day. Or no – a note that says we have to go somewhere. That way we won't be home to open the door." Miss Level looked at Petulia expectantly.

Petulia slowly raised her head and said, "That seems like a perfect idea. And I know just the place to find such a spell. Unfortunately, that place has mysteriously vanished."

At this Miss Level bit her bottom lip and cast a quick glance towards Gabriel, and then the door of the study.

"Anyway, who is to say that God wouldn't come back on a different day and we would still play the game?" Petulia lifted her shoulders in a half-shrug. "We can't go around sending ourselves thousands of notes every day." She sighed. "We will have to think of something else. Damn it."

Adam was lying on his back in the meadow he had come across. The sheepdog was lying a bit further away, whimpering. All the barking and jumping around he had done had been to no avail. The sheep were gone and the stranger was responsible. Now the dog only wanted the stranger to get it over with and eat him too. The dog felt that he deserved nothing less.

Adam, however, was completely satisfied. He looked up at the clouds and smiled. It would take a while before he would be able to get back up and continue his walk. So he would wait here to digest. Maybe sleep for a bit. He closed his eyes.

*

"Damn it. Enough of this. We can't just sit here and feel sorry for ourselves." Petulia pushed her chair back and stood up. "All right. I will check upstairs and you can check downstairs." She turned to go up the stairs.

"Check for what?" Miss Level frowned at her.

"For *The Big Book of Dale*, of course. As God predicted, it has all the answers so it might be able to get us out of this mess. Now, get busy." She motioned for Miss Level to get up and start searching. Then she turned and walked up the stairs.

Miss Level, still sitting at the table, looked at Gabriel. "Well, there goes my brilliant plan."

Gabriel just stared at her.

"I'll get up in a minute to go and fix the book." She gathered the teacups together. "Maybe she won't remember why we were looking for it in the first place." With a heavy heart she stood up and put the teacups in the sink. That's when Gabriel opened his mouth to speak – well, sing – some words of encouragement.

"*Thank you for trying, but I understand. I promise I won't start crying. I'll even lend a hand.*"

Miss Level turned to him and smiled; a sad little smile, but a smile nonetheless. They cleared the rest of the table together and then walked over to the study. Miss Level opened the door and walked in, and Gabriel followed close behind her.

Both were standing in front of the bookcase and stared at the now-empty spot on the shelf where *The Big Book of Dale* had been. Miss Level and Gabriel frowned, looked at each other and then back to the shelf.

"It was right here, wasn't it?" Miss Level pointed to the vacant spot.

Standing with their backs to the door, they did not notice the tiny, moss-green *Big Book of Dale* moving closer to the open door. The only sign that something was going on was a slight ticking on the floor, like tiny feet.

Just as *The Big Book of Dale* disappeared through the door, Miss Level turned and said, "I think we might have mice."

Tiny as *The Big Book of Dale* now was, it took a while for it to wiggle across the room. Of course, had it known then what it was going to know ten minutes later it would have moved a lot faster. Those ten minutes passed by as if in slow motion for the book, rounding obstacles like furniture to make it across the room. For Miss Level and Gabriel those minutes were spent searching for *The Big Book of Dale*. They even sank down on all fours to see if it had fallen down from the shelf somehow. Petulia, of course, had been upstairs, searching for it all along.

When the book reached the other side of the room after eight of those ten minutes, it was stopped in its tracks by the kitchen cupboards. It had noticed that the window near the sink was open and had formulated a plan, but unfortunately now it was stuck on the floor. It thought for a bit. Suddenly it dropped backwards on its spine, pages open for all to see. Then it started to flap its front and back covers. The object was not to rock itself back upright, but to fly. It took about two minutes for it to create the perfect rhythm, but gradually it started to achieve lift-off.

This was the moment Miss Level came out of the study. "I don't understand. I only meant to change it so Petulia wouldn't

43

find it. It cannot have disappeared. Maybe I don't know my own power."

She was vexed, until she noticed movement near the kitchen sink. It took her a while to realise it was a book, flying around the kitchen. It took her even longer to realise it was *The Big Book of Dale*. By the time the connection made it to her brain and her brain made her move her feet to stop the book from escaping, it was too late. Out the window it went. Miss Level made it to the window just in time to see it fly towards the east.

Gabriel had seen the whole thing and came to stand next to her at the window. He put his arm around Miss Level's shoulders.

"I didn't see that one coming. Can't say I'm very sad. But I'll refrain from humming, 'cause I know you probably feel bad."

"What are you two doing?" Petulia was standing at the top of the stairs. "Why aren't you looking for *The Big Book of Dale*?"

Miss Level and Gabriel froze. Both took a deep breath before turning around to face Petulia, who was coming down the stairs.

"Well, you see, uhmm…" Miss Level was at a loss for words.

"Yes?" Petulia had reached the bottom of the stairs and was now standing in her all-too-familiar pose, which was – on this occasion – accompanied by a slight tapping of her right foot.

Miss Level took a deep breath and decided to just get it over with. "Well, Gabriel was so sad about his horns and I didn't want him to be sad, so I cast a spell on *The Big Book of Dale* to transform it, which worked perfectly and it shrank and shrank and turned a mossy green kind of colour, and then we had tea and my ear started to itch and I knew it was important to have the book back…" Big breath. "So Gabriel and I went back into the study and looked and looked but it was gone, and then I heard this ticking sound and I thought we had mice so I didn't pay any attention to it and went back to looking for *The Big Book of Dale*, but then the ticking became a tapping and the tapping grew louder and louder and then it morphed into a kind of flapping." Another big breath. "So I came into the living room and saw *The Big Book of Dale* flying through the kitchen, and I ran to the window but it was too late and the book flew out and headed east." Final big breath.

Petulia stared with her mouth open. Then she looked at Gabriel, who just nodded his head in affirmation of this elaborate story. She looked back at Miss Level. "You did what?"

A little confused, Miss Level asked, "Do you really want me to repeat all that?"

Petulia's eyes narrowed. "Just give me the highlights again."

Hesitantly, Miss Level said, "Well, I transformed *The Big Book of Dale* with a spell so you wouldn't be able to find it, but then I realised we were going to need it because of my itching ear so we went to look for it but it wasn't on the shelf any more, and by the time I realised what was going on *The Big Book of Dale* had flown out the window." A short pause. "In a nutshell."

Petulia abandoned her usual pose and walked towards the coat rack near the front door. "Well then, I guess we are going book hunting." She put on a scarf and her coat, then took a hat and positioned it on her head.

Miss Level and Gabriel cast a quick glance at each other and decided it would be best just to do what Petulia wanted to. They both walked towards the coat rack. When Petulia noticed that

Gabriel was trying to wriggle himself into one of her coats, she mumbled, "That won't do," and said a few Latin words while pointing at him. Immediately a shirt covered his bare chest and the coat he was molesting transformed into a men's coat. "Good." She nodded.

She opened the door – "East, you said?" – and then walked outside, heading right. Miss Level and Gabriel quickly followed her.

Adam sat up and looked around. He was surprised to find the whimpering dog still lying close to him. He put his hand on the dog's head and scratched behind his ears. He realised this was a peculiar thing to do but could not make himself stop.

The sheepdog was just as surprised as he was. Although he still had a certain amount of fear for this strange man, he was glad to be scratched behind his ears. His real boss only hit him and locked him up. Come to think of it, where was his boss? The dog knew that his barking and jumping must have made quite a ruckus, so where was the evil farmer?

The dog decided not to care. With the sheep gone there was no more work for him on the farm anyway. He would just enjoy the attention his ears were getting from this stranger and then hope he wouldn't be eaten by said stranger too.

Adam still felt peculiar, scratching the dog's ears, but the motion had a kind of calming effect on him. He looked around and noticed a fence all around the meadow. Somehow – in his hungry state – he had jumped the fence without realising it.

On the other side, away from the forest, Adam suddenly

saw a road. He followed it with his eyes and could make out the outline of a city in the east.

He looked back at the dog, still scratching his ears. "Do you want to come?"

The dog opened his eyes at the sound of Adam's voice.

"I promise I won't eat you." Adam was surprised to find he actually meant those words. He stood up, wiped his hands on his waistcoat and walked away. When he noticed the dog wasn't following, he turned around and slapped his thigh. It seemed like a natural thing to do.

The dog stood up, looked to the west where the farm was, figured he would only get punished if he went back there and decided to risk going along with the stranger. He walked up to Adam and they went on their way, climbing over the fence – or under it in the dog's case – in the direction of the mysterious city.

Five

The Search for The Big Book of Dale

Petulia was walking swiftly down a worn path with Miss Level and Gabriel in tow. She kept craning her neck up, watching for any movement up above. But all those damned trees were in the way. The sky made an appearance only sporadically. At least she knew that they would come to a clearing soon.

Miss Level was racked with guilt. Because of this she kept her head down, which was a good thing, otherwise she would never have noticed the inch-wide black spot in the grass. She stopped abruptly, which made Gabriel bump into her – he had been looking up because Petulia was looking up and this seemed like the right thing to do. But now he stopped. He didn't know why Miss Level had stopped and looked ahead at Petulia, who still had her head raised up towards the sky.

"Petulia, hang on, please. Stop and turn around. You can come back with ease. She's found something on the ground."

Petulia turned around and saw Miss Level bent over investigating something. "Did you turn *The Big Book of Dale* into a tiny, puny little thing the size of an ant?" She walked back towards

Miss Level and Gabriel. By the time she reached them Gabriel had also bent down, and Miss Level was on her haunches. "Because, if you did, this will be worse than that needle we once looked for. Remember that?" Mumbling, "Bloody haystack."

"No," said Miss Level, frowning, "it's something else." She waved her hand at Petulia. "Look at this. This doesn't seem right."

Overwhelmed by curiosity, Petulia also bent down. All three of them stared at the blacked-out piece of grass.

"How peculiar," Miss Level mused. "I don't know any other word for it." Then, more to herself, "But what does it mean?"

"It's just a tiny patch of soot. Blow at it and it will probably go away." Petulia wasn't the most patient woman in the world and had already turned around to continue on her quest when she heard Miss Level blowing.

"Well, you were wrong. The earth here is scorched." Miss Level rummaged through her bag and found a small box, the size of a box of matches. She picked up the remaining soot and put it in the box. Then she dropped the box in her bag and stood up. Gabriel followed suit. Petulia had already created quite a distance between them, so they hurried to catch up with her.

The tops of the trees got leafier and it was harder to see the sky. Petulia figured *The Big Book of Dale* wouldn't stay around for that long anyway, so she looked ahead and navigated through the forest. Miss Level's mind was still preoccupied with the ashes they had stumbled upon. She wondered what could make such a small scorch mark and what it was that had been scorched.

Gabriel just followed the two women because he didn't know what else to do. He was delighted to be out of the house and into the forest. The forest had left a great impression on him and he couldn't stop looking around and taking in all the details. He saw squirrels fighting over nuts, birds tumbling over each other in the sky and a rabbit hopping away from them. He was enthralled by all the noises he could hear: the tapping of a woodpecker's beak against the bark of a tree, the love song the tumbling birds were producing and the gentle rustle of the leaves as the wind washed through them.

When they neared the meadow, Petulia started looking up again. No flying books anywhere. Miss Level and Gabriel, who had by then caught up with her, were walking like normal people, with their heads turned forward. That is why they were the first to see the meadow and the unfortunate carnage of dead sheep. All they could do was stop and stare.

Now it was Petulia's turn to bump into someone and she did so expertly – Miss Level and Gabriel slammed into the fence surrounding the meadow.

"Damn it. Keep moving," Petulia said. It was only after she had uttered that last sentence that she looked down and saw what the others were seeing. "What the…?"

"What are those things?" Miss Level had tilted her head sideways but could not even guess what the heaps of bones had been.

Petulia squinted. "I think they were sheep."

"What happened to them?"

"If I had to guess, I would say something ate them." Petulia was her usual pragmatic self and didn't seem to have any trouble with finding piles of chewed sheep in a meadow.

Gabriel, who was still new to this world, feared that they

might be attacked by a crazed animal and started shifting uncomfortably on his feet. His head swung back and forth, taking in the forest he once thought beautiful. Now it looked dark and uninviting. He pressed closer to Miss Level.

In any other circumstances Miss Level would have welcomed the hard body of a full-grown man pressing against her backside. Now, however, she was a bit preoccupied trying to figure out what could have done this. Confronted with two mysteries in such a short space of time, her mind did not know which to tackle first, so it tackled both at the same time but could not make the link between them. Confused, she turned towards Petulia.

Petulia herself had decided that there was nothing they could do for the mauled sheep and was walking along the fence to the nearby gate in the middle of it. Miss Level didn't want to be left alone with the chewed-up sheep, so she hurried to catch up with her. Those were Gabriel's sentiments as well, so he ran along beside her towards Petulia.

"What are we going to do?"

"We are looking for *The Big Book of Dale* and after we find it we are going to see what we can do about this game we are playing with God and maybe get rid of Gabriel's horns." Petulia opened the gate and walked into the meadow.

Gabriel had actually forgotten the original plan concerning *The Big Book of Dale* and his horns. He was surprised to hear Petulia mention destroying his horns so matter-of-factly. Still, the idea of being alone was more terrifying at this moment than losing his horns. He swallowed his pride and continued to follow the two women.

"That is not what I meant," Miss Level said. "What are we going to do about the sheep?"

Petulia stopped and turned towards her, frowning. "Nothing. What is done is done." With these words she turned around again and walked on.

"Shouldn't we bury them or something?"

Petulia waved her hand towards Miss Level. "If you want to bury them, you can, but I'm not waiting for you." She continued to cross the meadow.

Miss Level halted, which made Gabriel stop as well – he liked Miss Level a lot better than Petulia and would much rather stay close to her. She closed her eyes and mumbled a few words in Latin. The ground beneath each carcass started to move and slowly the bones began to sink into the earth. The only sign that anything had happened were the giant molehills that had appeared. Miss Level opened her eyes again, was happy with the result and tugged Gabriel's arm so he would follow her across the meadow.

Petulia had already reached the other side. She looked around swiftly – not wanting to take her eyes off the sky for too long – and nodded her approval at Miss Level's burial work. She opened the second gate in the fence and stood on the road. Looking left and right, she was debating her options. Well, actually she was trying to think like a book. Where would a book go if it were free to go wherever it wanted to? She figured it would probably want to be near its own kind, so she turned left and walked towards the city. Unfortunately, a book doesn't really think that much; it already has all the knowledge it could need within its pages. Even *The Big Book of Dale* was on nothing more than a mindless trip and so it hadn't gone left or right, but had just flown straight ahead.

Adam was getting closer to the city, with the scruffy-looking dog still following right behind him. He had hoped to see more of the city the closer he came, but it was surrounded by a high and thick wall. There was a gate at the end of the road, which was guarded by a person who would have been long retired if he had lived in our world. The guard was wearing chain mail and a helmet that was a tad too big, and carried a spear.

"Halt!" The shaky voice of the elderly man was no threat to Adam. Even the lowering of the spear was useless – granted, it took about two minutes for the spear to be lowered to waist height. Then the visor of the helmet clanked down and the image was complete.

Adam's right eyebrow lifted. "Yes?"

The old guard raised the spear again, held it with one hand – which seemed to be very tricky – and lifted the visor with his other hand. "What?" Apparently his hearing had seen better days as well.

"What do you want?" Adam had never encountered a deaf person before, so he did not know he had to raise his voice to be heard properly.

"WHAT?" The deaf guard did know he had to raise his voice, and was on the verge of shouting.

Adam frowned, hesitated and then shouted back. "WHAT DO YOU WANT?" He figured it might be a custom he was unaware of.

"I'm supposed to ask you that." The guard's false teeth created a lisp to accompany these words. "What do you want?"

"I want to enter this great city." Adam waved his hand in the direction of the city, just in case the old man might not know which city he meant. "Pray tell, what is the name of this fair city?"

"What?" The old man was cupping his hand near his ear.

"What – is – the – name – of – this – city?" Adam finally realisunderstood what the problem was and decided that good articulation might go a long way.

"Clariceville." The guard realised that the man in front of him was a stranger, and felt the need to elaborate. "It used to be called Edmundtown but then he died and his daughter took over, so she had the name changed." He checked over his shoulder to see if anybody was standing there. Then he leaned forward, which made Adam lean forward as well, out of curiosity. "A bit of an egotistical lady, if you ask me." The guard stood back, lowered his spear again and said, "Now, why are you here?"

Adam shrugged. "Just visiting."

"What?" The visor clanked down again when the old man tilted his head to hear better.

"VISITING!"

"Visiting who?"

Adam shook his head. "I'm just visiting the city."

"What?" He lifted the visor.

"VISITING THE CITY!" Adam's throat was beginning to hurt from all the shouting. Keep in mind that he had never shouted before.

"Business or pleasure?" The guard lifted the spear again so he could lean on it for a bit. His back was killing him.

"Uhm…pleasure, I guess." Adam wasn't really sure what to answer. He hadn't thought about why he wanted to visit the city; he just knew that he did.

"What?" Clank!

"PLEASURE!" He was beginning to become fed up with the guard – and let's face it, Adam fed up was not a pretty picture.

"Well, why didn't you say so?" The old man lifted the visor while he rested his spear against the wall. He picked up a satchel and went through it. "Hang on. Now where is it?" He rummaged on while Adam controlled the urge to tap his feet or just jump on the man and eat him. The only thing stopping him was that the man was clearly older than the lady he had eaten the day before and would most likely be even harder to digest.

"Here it is." He handed Adam a piece of paper that had been neatly folded several times. "That's a map of the city. In case you lose it, if you get lost you can just focus on the tower of the castle. It's the ugly pink thing in the centre of the city. You can't miss it." And with those words he waved Adam through the gate.

Petulia kept her nose in the air while Miss Level and Gabriel just looked around. Miss Level showed him all the new things he had never seen before. She pointed at the babbling brook that seemed to follow them on their trip and told him it was called the New Brook but it had been around for a hundred years.

Miss Level remembered very well when the brook first appeared. It had been a hot summer day and all the people had stayed inside because the heat was just too much. But Miss Level had gone out to get some herbs so she could dry them and try out a new tea combination. She was the only one to hear a soft whining noise. As curious as she was, she went in search of the origin of the noise. That's when she met Althea.

Althea was a mountain troll. She had left her country a few days earlier in search of her love, but had been unsuccessful in finding him. All of a sudden she had begun to wonder if he actually wanted to be found, and now she was angry and scared and so far from home that she had just stopped and sat down. Emotion overwhelming her, she started to cry. Miss Level had tried to calm her down and cheer her up but it was no use. Althea decided to stay where she was, blending into her surroundings. Now you couldn't see where Althea ended and the ground began; she had become one with the earth. The constant stream of tears and the soft whining sounds were the only indications that she was still there.

When Miss Level had finished her story she noticed Gabriel regarding her with a doubtful look in his eyes.

"I know what you're thinking. Why still call it the New Brook when the origin of the brook is known?"

Gabriel just nodded.

"Well, I didn't really tell anyone about Althea except Petulia. But I know she can keep a secret and I think you can too."

Again, Gabriel nodded.

"I didn't want people to go up to her and make fun of her or start poking her. Being a troll doesn't mean you don't have feelings. You would be surprised to find out how emotional trolls can get. Especially the female ones."

Then she pointed to a golden flower, told Gabriel it was called a narcissus and talked about a guy who had been so vain he had turned into a flower. Gabriel was finding it hard to believe everything Miss Level was telling him, but at least the time went by more quickly and she could really tell a tale.

When they first entered the city, Adam and the dog were hit by the smell of it. It smelled like rotten eggs, stale beer and smelly feet. Not the best combination to welcome strangers.

They walked down what appeared to be the main street. The smell gradually changed to that of cooked meat, which made Adam hungry again. The dog wasn't unaffected either. At least Adam realised he was in the city and that it was daytime, so he repressed his baser instincts and walked on.

The dog, however, really wanted something to eat. He stopped regularly to sniff at doorways and windows. When Adam realised what was going on, he called the dog to him and they went into a tavern called The Last Call.

That was about the time Petulia, Miss Level and Gabriel reached the gate of the city. The old guard had started to lower his spear when he spotted the three of them coming around the bend. It was almost at waist height when they stopped in front of him.

"Halt!" he said with his shaky voice.

"HI, GERALD. HOW ARE YOU?" Miss Level frequently visited the city and knew the man very well. Unfortunately his memory was fading fast and they had to get reacquainted every time she passed him.

"How do you know my name?" Gerald was a very suspicious man and the fading memory really wasn't helping things. "And why are you here?"

Petulia rolled her eyes at Miss Level and motioned for her to speed things up. Of course this wasn't possible when dealing with Gerald.

"IT'S ME, MISS LEVEL. WE NEED TO GET INTO THE CITY, GERALD."

"What? Who are you?" The tilting of his head made the visor clank down.

"MISS LEVEL! I HELPED YOU WITH YOUR HAEMOR-RHOID PROBLEM. REMEMBER?" Miss Level made a rubbing motion in the air. "I GOT YOU THAT GREAT SALVE."

Gerald, who was very shy about things that went on under-neath his clothes, immediately blushed and started to stutter – which made his words even more indiscernible because his visor was still down. "Wha-what do you wa-want in the ci-city to-today?"

Miss Level figured he was still asking what they wanted, so she just answered, "JUST LOOKING FOR SOMETHING."

Of course Gerald hadn't heard a word of what Miss Level had said, so he lifted the visor. "What?"

"LOOKING FOR SOMETHING."

"Business or pleasure?"

This was the moment when Petulia had had quite enough and decided to interfere. "Business," she said at the same time as Miss Level shouted, "PLEASURE."

The old man regarded both women, then looked at the

strange young man behind them with the curious hat on and asked, "Well, which is it?"

"BUSINESS," shouted Miss Level, while Petulia yelled, "PLEASURE!"

The old guard shook his head. "Ladies, you will have to make up your minds before I let you in."

Miss Level, who was a little annoyed that Petulia had tried to take over anyway, shushed her and turned to Gerald. "PLEASURE!"

Gerald looked at Petulia, who just nodded. Then he glanced at Gabriel. He too just nodded.

"Well then, let's see." Gerald put his spear against the wall and bent down for his satchel. He rummaged through it and finally came up with a paper, carefully folded several times, which he handed to Miss Level. "It's a map of the city. In case you lose it, if you get lost you can focus on the tower of the castle. It's the ugly pink thing in the centre of the city. You can't miss it." And with those words he waved the three of them through the gate.

Six

In the City

When they stepped through the gate, Petulia immediately started breathing through her mouth. She didn't like the city. The smell alone was enough, but all those people wandering around, being busy, yelling at each other, were just too much. And the fact that they threw their garbage on the street like that… Hadn't these people ever heard of recycling? Or hygiene for that matter?

That's why she always sent Miss Level whenever they had business in the city. Or why she told the people who wanted to procure their services to come to their house in the woods because of the privacy it would give them. Of course this meant that the only one of their little group who actually knew the way was Miss Level. And she was also the one with the map.

"We need to get to the library. I think that's our best chance of finding *The Big Book of Dale*." Petulia was seconds away from squeezing her nose shut with her fingers.

"All right. Follow me." Miss Level walked straight ahead, not seeming to notice all the filth lying on the ground. Petulia, however, tiptoed around every morsel of non-earth she could see.

Gabriel didn't really look where he put his feet. He was too busy looking around. He liked the forest more than the city, but he was curious about all those people. When they passed a tavern on the right, he could see a scruffy-looking dog lying in front of it. It was the first time he had seen a dog. What a weird-looking creature. But then a cat went racing past the dog and Gabriel's attention went with it.

The dog had been sent outside. Who knew a dog was not allowed in a tavern – even a filthy tavern like this one? So now the dog was lying outside, waiting for the stranger. Truth be told, he was happy to wait outside. He had noticed how the stranger had been looking at the fat owner of the tavern. Let's just say he seemed to be the tastiest thing on the menu. The dog was happy that he wouldn't have to see his new master's eating habits again.

He lifted his head. New master? Oh, crap. Had he bonded with this weird man? This would not bode well.

The dog looked to his right and saw two strange-looking women and a tall man round the corner. Nothing special about that, but the dog had a feeling he would see that trio again in the not-too-distant future.

The stranger came out of the tavern with a bowl of water and a bowl of stew. He put them down in front of the dog, patted his head and said, "We will be here for a while. Get comfortable." Then he disappeared through the door again.

Well, at least the dog was happy to get fed. A big improvement on his last master. Shit, there was that word again.

*

When they rounded the corner, Miss Level noticed that the hairs on the back of her neck had stood up while they were walking down that last street. She hesitated for a while, wondering if she should go back and find out where that warning sign was coming from.

"Don't tell me you have already lost your way?" Petulia assumed her usual pose.

"No, I just—"

"We don't have all day," Petulia interrupted. "The sooner we find *The Big Book of Dale*, the sooner we can clean up this mess." She walked past Miss Level in the direction they had been going.

Miss Level looked back for a while but decided to keep heading for the library as planned. If it was something serious she would have had a bigger warning than the hairs on the back of her neck standing up, right? She tried to shrug off the feeling of menace and continued on.

Petulia had come to a crossroads and was waiting for Miss Level to catch up. She tried to make it look like she was just waiting for Miss Level instead of what was really going on – she had no idea where the hell she was. Still in the city, that was for sure. She pulled out a handkerchief and pressed it over her nose and mouth.

Miss Level and Gabriel caught up. Then Miss Level turned left and the other two followed. Up ahead loomed the castle of Princess Clarice. Petulia had to agree with the old guard at the gate: it really was a big, ugly pink thing and very hard to miss. Why on earth would anybody paint his or her house – or castle – a ghastly shade of fuchsia?

When they reached the outer wall of the castle Miss Level

turned right and followed the wall to the end. Then she continued straight until they reached a big, classic brick building: the library.

"Now, we don't have a library card so we will have to register if we want to search the building. Are you sure *The Big Book of Dale* will be here?" Miss Level asked Petulia.

"Of course I am sure." Petulia was surprised that Miss Level questioned her actions and logic; she had never done so before. She would just have to prove that she was right and everything would go back to normal. Petulia walked past Miss Level and entered the library.

Miss Level watched Gabriel, who seemed to be in awe of the building they were standing in front of. She was happy that he had come into their lives. He made her realise that there was a lot of beauty in the world that she had started to take for granted. She stepped up next to him, turned around and looked at the library building, trying to see it as Gabriel was seeing it.

It was a fine piece of architecture. The red bricks were complemented by sandstone around the windows and as a border at the top of the building. The big wooden door looked so heavy it seemed like it would have to be opened by a giant, but the carvings in the wood were gorgeous: cherubs, humans, elves, trolls and other creatures all sitting and reading. The archway over the door was made from the same sandstone and had an inscription that read: *Venient in et quiescatisí*, which just meant, *Come in and be quiet*, but it seemed more important in Latin.

Petulia came back out and saw them standing there like a pair of idiots. "Damn it. Will you two hurry up?" She disappeared back inside.

Miss Level and Gabriel looked at each other, smiled and shrugged. Then both of them entered the big building. They stepped into a huge hallway. The ceiling was high above them and had a painting on it that reached from corner to corner. Again, all sorts of creatures were depicted, sitting and reading. On the right side of the hallway was a reception area. Petulia was already standing there. When Miss Level and Gabriel finished taking in the ceiling, they walked over to the reception desk.

Petulia turned to Miss Level. "This insipid woman will not help me." Her hands found her hips again while she glared at the relatively young woman behind the desk.

"It must be your sunny disposition," Miss Level mumbled. She walked up to the desk and stood in front of Petulia to block her from the receptionist's view.

"Hello," a quick glance at the woman's name tag, "Julia. May I call you Julia?"

"It's my name, isn't it?" Julia replied while chewing gum.

Miss Level smiled at her. "Excuse my friend here. She has been having a bad day."

At this Petulia snorted. Miss Level elbowed her to keep her quiet.

"We would like to go inside and take a look around. If that's all right with you?"

"You need a pass. I tried to tell your *friend* that," emphasis on 'friend', "but she just started calling me names."

Petulia stuck her head out from behind Miss Level. "We just want to look around. We're not going to take anything." Miss Level tried to shove her back.

"Well, you still need a pass," Julia said testily. Then she looked at Miss Level. "It's regulation. The guard won't let you in otherwise." As she said this, she pointed to something behind them.

Gabriel, Petulia and Miss Level turned their heads to see what she was pointing at. A tall and very broad man was standing at the door leading into the library, checking everybody who tried to get in. Three gulps resounded in the hallway.

"Well, we have no problem applying for a library card." Miss Level elbowed Petulia again. "Now do we?"

Petulia gasped, but nodded obediently.

Julia smiled. "Good. Fill out these forms first. There is a table to your left where you can sit and find some pens. Then come back here and we'll take it from there." She handed them a stack of papers and then turned back to what she had been doing before Petulia had so rudely interrupted.

The three companions sat down at the table and Miss Level handed out the forms. They each grabbed a pen and stared at the first page. Miss Level and Petulia stared because the questions were just plain weird, and Gabriel stared because he couldn't read, let alone write.

Adam had taken one look at the fat tavern owner and his mouth started to water again. How could he be so hungry? It hadn't been that long ago since he had eaten several sheep.

The dog had taken one look at Adam's face and knew what was going to happen next. The fat tavern owner had taken one look at the dog and ordered Adam to take him outside. At this

65

the dog had seemed relieved, so Adam nodded to him and he had left the tavern.

Knowing the dog was hungry too, Adam had ordered some water and stew and taken it outside. Now he was sitting at his table in the corner with a glass of ale in front of him. Adam decided he liked ale. It would go well with some meat, though. He glanced at the fat tavern owner. He needed a plan to get the man alone. He was pretty sure that eating a person would be frowned upon by the other people.

Adam glared at every person in the tavern, willing them to leave. He was surprised to find that this actually worked. Every single person in the tavern quickly finished their meal, downed their drink and left.

The owner was surprised to suddenly find his tavern almost empty. He regarded the man sitting in the corner and figured he could handle one client by himself.

"Mary, you can take off. Rush hour is done."

The waitress was very happy with this news, immediately took off her apron and hurried outside in case the owner changed his mind.

The owner waddled up to where Adam was sitting. "Can I get you anything else?"

Adam smiled. "I would like to eat something, but I am very particular about the sort of meat I eat. Could I see what you have in your kitchen?"

The owner frowned. Nobody had ever requested to see his kitchen before. It was a mess in there, but if that was what the customer wanted, then that was what the customer would get.

"Follow me."

Adam stood and followed the fat man into the back. When they passed the counter, he grabbed a knife and fork – he was going to see if utensils actually made things easier or not – and stuffed the tip of a napkin in the collar of his shirt.

"Why do they need to know what my favourite food is?" Petulia asked. "What does that have to do with books?"

Miss Level agreed. "And why do they need to know what kind of underwear we wear? That's none of their business." She looked at the paper with all the questions. At least the questions were multiple choice. "I'm just going to tick the *All of the above* boxes."

"Sounds like a plan." Petulia bent over the paper and started to check all the boxes on the right side.

Gabriel, who still hadn't been able to fill in anything – not even his name – saw what Petulia was doing, noticed that Miss Level had started to do the same thing and figured, what the hell? He shrugged and started ticking boxes as well. When they were done Miss Level gathered the papers and quickly wrote down Gabriel's name when she noticed he had left that blank. Then the three of them stood up and walked back to the reception desk.

"Finished?" Julia grabbed their papers, didn't even glance at them and just fed them into a machine. It buzzed and peeped for about five minutes and then finally spewed out three laminated cards. Julia picked them up.

"Miss Level?"

Miss Level lifted her hand and Julia gave her one of the cards. "Petulia?"

Petulia lifted her hand and also received a card.

"And Gabriel?"

Gabriel stepped forward and stuck out his hand to receive his own card.

Julia held it out to him, batted her eyelashes and said, "Welcome, Gabriel. I hope you enjoy the library."

Gabriel smiled at her in response and tugged at the card, but Julia wouldn't let go and kept batting her eyes at him.

Miss Level yanked the card out of Julia's hand. "I am sure *we* will." Then she grabbed Gabriel's hand and pulled him towards the entrance to the library.

Gabriel didn't quite understand what was going on, but followed Miss Level obediently. He glanced back at Julia, who was still standing at the desk, pouting. Petulia walked right behind them, smiling. She had finally realised what was going on with her friend, and was very amused.

"Passes!" They had reached the guard who was blocking the entrance – double doors. All three of them held up their new cards.

The guard rolled his eyes and pointed at a little black box next to the door. "Passes!"

Miss Level looked at the others and shrugged. She stepped up to the little black box and slid her card through the slit in the top of the box. A green light flashed and the guard waved her through. Petulia and Gabriel tried to follow her, but walked straight into the guard. He pointed at the box again.

"Passes!"

Both of them swiped their cards as well, resulting in the green light flashing. They were both allowed to enter the library. The moment they walked through the double doors the guard immediately turned his back on them.

Petulia, Miss Level and Gabriel looked around in amazement. They had never seen so many books in one place – especially Gabriel. The library consisted of several floors. From the doorway they could see all of the floors – seven in total – and all of them had books stacked from floor to ceiling, racks and racks of them.

"So," Miss Level whispered, "where do you suggest we begin?"

Petulia's mouth was still hanging open. She hadn't thought there would be this many books, so she hadn't foreseen any trouble. But this, this was overwhelming. They would need at least a month to go over every rack. What were they going to do? They didn't have a month.

"Well?" Miss Level whispered.

"Uhm…maybe we should start on the left side and work our way through to the right?" Petulia had no idea if this was a good method but it was the only one that came to mind at that moment.

Miss Level shrugged. "All right." She headed towards the children's section with Gabriel right behind her.

Petulia stood frozen for a while longer. Maybe this hadn't been such a good idea after all. Maybe they should have just waited at home. Maybe *The Big Book of Dale* had just wanted to stretch its pages for a bit and had already returned to the house.

Miss Level turned and hissed, "Petulia!" which resulted in

several people lifting their heads and shushing her. When Petulia looked over, Miss Level signalled for her to follow. Knowing that Petulia had never been in a library before, she was pretty sure her friend would get lost if left by herself. Unhurriedly, Petulia obeyed.

Adam walked out of the tavern, buttoning up his waistcoat. He was having some trouble with the buttons at his waist. He pulled the lapels closer together and popped the last one.

The dog lifted his head. Adam closed the door behind him and looked around.

"Which way should we go?"

The dog stood up and turned to his right. He started to walk that way, but Adam stopped him.

"Didn't we come from that direction?"

The dog barked.

"I don't want to leave the city yet. We haven't even seen anything worthwhile. Let's go this way." Adam turned left and strolled down the street.

The dog shook his head, but followed anyway. He had a feeling that the stranger was going to get himself into trouble. He might as well try and keep him out of it.

Seven

Searching in the Library

"This is just ridiculous." Miss Level looked up from the seventh bookcase she had investigated. They had been in the library for half an hour and had only managed to check a tiny portion of the children's area.

"Well, what do you suggest?" Petulia glared at her.

"We are witches," Miss Level whispered in reply, "and we are looking for a magic book. Why don't we try – what's it called – magic?"

"Damn it, that's what got us here in the first place."

"That was just a side effect I hadn't counted on." Miss Level was becoming angry and purple again.

Petulia shoved her behind a rack of books. "Look, it doesn't matter. We just have to find the book and then we can get out of here."

The purple glow Miss Level was giving off was not diminishing.

"If you think we can find the book easier with a spell, we can try it. But we have to be careful."

The glow started to disappear. Petulia didn't really know what would happen if Miss Level kept getting angrier and angrier but she figured that the purple glow wasn't a good sign so she always tried to calm her down when it appeared. Unfortunately this occasionally meant that she had to agree to do stuff that she really didn't want to do. Like now, for instance – she really thought it wasn't a good idea to use magic in a library full of people. But would it be better to blow up the library, if that happened to be a side effect of the purple glow?

"I have an idea." Petulia kept her hands on Miss Level's shoulders as she spoke. "Why don't we wait for nightfall to try a spell? That way there won't be any people around. What do you say?"

Miss Level thought for a while and then saw the logic of this idea. She nodded her approval. "Why don't we go and have something to eat while we decide what spell to use?" she suggested.

Petulia smiled at her – mostly glad that the purple glow was now completely gone, but also feeling a little famished – and nodded. Gabriel – who remembered how good those cookies had tasted – immediately nodded as well and the three of them left the library in search of a tavern.

It didn't take too long. Right across the street was a cosy little coffee-and-cake shop. They went in and sat down in one of the corners.

The waitress immediately came to their table. "Hello and welcome to Granny's Coffee and Cake Shop. Here is our menu. Take a look and just wave when you know what you would like."

She handed over the menus, smiled and returned to the counter.

All three of them simultaneously opened their menus and studied the goodies on offer. Luckily for Gabriel, there were pictures. The Belgian waffles looked good.

"Do you think they would mind if I made my own tea?" Miss Level asked.

Petulia didn't even look up. "I am fairly certain that they would. Just pick something from the menu."

Miss Level pouted. She wanted to see if she could make the same tea as before. "All right," she sighed, "I'll just have some camomile tea with a slice of rhubarb pie."

"Do you know what you would like, Gabriel?" Petulia wanted to keep him from singing. "Just point it out to me and I'll order."

Gabriel was happy with this arrangement and quickly pointed to the Belgian waffles, strawberry shortcake and hot cocoa. Petulia waved at the waitress, who promptly left her seat behind the counter and sauntered over to their table.

"We will have a pot of camomile tea with two cups, a slice of rhubarb pie, a slice of chocolate cake, a stack of Belgian waffles, a strawberry shortcake and a cup of hot cocoa." Petulia regarded the waitress. "Shouldn't you write this down?"

"Nope, got it." The waitress summed up everything while extending her fingers one by one. "Camomile tea, one pot, two cups. Rhubarb pie, chocolate cake, each one slice. Belgian waffles, strawberry shortcake and hot cocoa. Would you like whipped cream on the cocoa?"

Gabriel beamed at the waitress. He had no idea what whipped cream was but it sounded delicious. Not wanting to embarrass his companions, he just nodded vigorously.

"Anything else?"

"No thank you." Petulia handed back her menu; the two others followed her example. The chipper waitress spun around and returned to the counter. She immediately busied herself with preparing their order.

"Any idea on how to find *The Big Book of Dale* in that library?" Petulia asked nonchalantly.

Miss Level thought about it for a while and really wished she hadn't put that spell on the book. Life would be so much easier if they had *The Big Book of Dale* right now. She started to feel guilty, and wasn't even sure why she had transformed it in the first place. Then she glanced at Gabriel and remembered. He was wearing a hat now, but she knew the unmistakable horns were still there. Gabriel felt her gaze upon him and looked up.

Petulia noticed what was going on and decided to nip it in the bud. "I think we should just try a standard locator spell."

Miss Level's gaze immediately snapped to meet Petulia's.

"We could adjust it a little to aim for *The Big Book of Dale*. Just trying to locate a book in a library would be pretty stupid. How can we focus the spell?"

"We should probably use a focusing tool," Miss Level suggested. "Which means we need water, earth, fire or wind." She bent down and rummaged through her bag. When she straightened up, she was holding a box of matches. "Maybe if we use two of them – like we did when we created Gabriel – it will work even better."

That didn't sound like such a dumb idea, so Petulia agreed.

"Do you have a piece of paper and some charcoal in that bag of yours?"

Miss Level went through her bag again and came up with a flyer from the theatre and the ashes she found in the forest. "This is the best I can do." She handed everything over to Petulia.

Petulia turned over the flyer to write on the back. Then she stuck her pinkie finger in the ashes and wrote *Big Book of Dale*. Just to be sure, she also wrote *magic book*. You never know, there might be another book out there with the same name. This way, even if they located the wrong book, it would still be a book of magic.

"All right. This looks good." Petulia folded the piece of paper in two and put it next to her on the table. She placed the box of matches on top of it.

Just then the waitress showed up with their drinks. The pot of camomile tea was placed in the middle of the table and both Miss Level and Petulia received a cup. A big mug filled with hot cocoa was placed in front of Gabriel. The waitress took out a special device and squirted whipped cream on top of it – it kind of looked like a hat. Gabriel's eyes opened wide and he greedily grabbed a spoon to start. The waitress smiled and went back to the counter for the rest of their order.

Gabriel was just scooping up his first spoonful of whipped cream when the waitress put a plate with a stack of Belgian waffles in front of him. The smell worked wonders and he absently put the spoon of whipped cream in his mouth while looking at the steaming waffles and the accompanying strawberry shortcake.

The sweetness of the whipped cream exploded in his mouth. He moaned. He couldn't help it – he just moaned.

The three women were looking at him, amazed at his wonder. When the waitress finally put the slice of rhubarb pie in front of Miss Level and the piece of chocolate cake in front of Petulia, they were smiling and looking forward to the same sweet experience as Gabriel was having. The waitress went back to the counter and took a piece of cake for herself, just to see if she could still be as amazed and surprised by the taste as Gabriel.

In his enthusiasm to get to the waffles quickly he accidently knocked the pot of tea. It didn't fall over, but a slight spillage of tea did happen. Petulia immediately grabbed her napkin and patted the table dry. Unfortunately, none of them noticed that some of the tea had made its way to the folded paper.

Finally Petulia put her little fork down, still savouring the last lingering taste of chocolatey goodness. She picked up her cup of tea and sipped. Unwittingly, Miss Level mirrored her exact movements. After ravaging the last of the Belgian waffles, Gabriel leant back and scooted down a bit in his chair. They sat like that for about five minutes, satisfied and in companionable silence.

Miss Level sighed. "We should probably get going. The library will close in about half an hour."

"Yes, we probably should." But neither of them made any effort to get up. Eventually it was Gabriel who sat up straight and hinted at getting up – by actually getting up. Miss Level and Petulia grudgingly followed.

*

When they got back into the library – I will save you the skit with the guard – they walked up the stairs and went to the section marked *Divers*. There, Petulia took out the piece of paper and the box of matches. Miss Level and Gabriel stepped back and let her do what she needed to do.

With a lot of ceremony, Petulia took a match, lit it on the box and then dropped the box on the floor. She held the flame to the folded piece of paper.

I now invoke the air and fire,
Help me find what I desire.
I now invoke the air and fire,
Help me find what I desire.
I now invoke the air and fire,
Help me find what I desire.

With those last three words she released the burning paper. It was lifted into the air, where it danced around before falling apart in sparkling fragments. A chill was immediately felt throughout the library. The receptionist even wondered if someone had left a door open. Then the hum of vibration resounded. It grew louder and louder, and all the books in the library started to shake.

Suddenly one book flew across the room and smacked into the back of Petulia's head. Then another – and another – until she was sprawled on the floor, engulfed under a pile of books.

"I think we might have done something wrong," Miss Level hazarded while she started picking up the books that were burying Petulia.

The Big Book of Dale itself was still heading east when it suddenly felt a tug, pulling it to the south. Not being the thinking kind of book, it just went with the flow and changed direction.

Miss Level read the titles of all the books she was picking up. "Although they are all magic books."

The muffled sound of Petulia's voice came from the bottom of the pile. "I am thrilled." The pile started to quake, and then her left hand appeared. Gabriel immediately grabbed it and pulled it to free her. Petulia dusted herself off and stared angrily at the pile of books at her feet.

Miss Level felt that she should say something. "At least we have expedited our search. Now we won't have to look at every bookcase in this place." She glanced at Petulia, who was not amused. "I bet every magic book in the library is in that pile."

Just then they heard a crash. A window broke, and three more books hit Petulia in the head, which made her topple over, right on top of the pile of books.

"Maybe even a few that weren't from the library." Miss Level had trouble keeping a straight face when she saw Petulia rubbing the back of her head, her face all scrunched up. You have to realise that most magic books are not small. Most even come in several thick volumes because one just wouldn't be enough. It was exactly one of those examples that hit her the last time – three volumes of one book. At least it wasn't the extended version...

*

Adam was walking down the street when he suddenly felt peculiar. He couldn't really describe what he was feeling. First there was a chill, and then it seemed like he had goosebumps on the inside. Strange…

He was standing in the middle of the street, trying to figure out what was going on, when the dog started to bark at the sky. Adam looked up and saw a book flying through the air right above them. What was all that about?

The weird feeling in his stomach subsided. He bent down and patted the dog on the head. "You felt it too, right?"

The dog just watched him, silent now that the book had passed.

"Do you even have a name?" Adam scratched the dog behind his ears. "I should probably give you one if we are going to continue to hang out."

He thought for a bit. "How about Shep?"

The dog just watched him, enjoying the attention his ears were getting.

"I know, it's not very original, but I have never given a name to anything before. I think, for my first attempt, that it's not too bad. What do you think, Shep?"

The dog barked. He didn't really mind being called Shep. It was better than his last name: Fluffy. No idea how or why they came up with that one. It didn't work, either. The dog had consistently resisted answering to the name Fluffy. Shep, on the other hand, sounded all right. He would definitely answer to Shep.

Adam stood up. "Well, that's settled then. What do you say we move on, Shep?"

The dog barked once in affirmation and walked next to Adam down the road, passing a giant red-brick building which looked amazing, except for the broken window on the second floor.

Petulia was hiding out under a table in the library. She was fed up with being assaulted by magic books. A loud thump resounded when another one hit the tabletop. A little further away, Miss Level and Gabriel were sorting through the pile of books. She had explained to him to only keep the tiny moss-green ones or the big flashy red ones. The pile was getting smaller and smaller. However, the table under which Petulia was hiding was gradually getting fuller and fuller. Regrettably, neither Miss Level nor Gabriel wanted to go near that table, for fear of becoming collateral damage. At least the books in the pile on the floor were keeping quiet.

"This would go a lot faster if you would help us."

"And risk being beheaded by *An Encyclopaedia of Magicians*? I don't think so." Petulia put her hands against the tabletop. It had started to buckle under the weight. She might have to seek another spot for protection.

"What's all this banging?" The receptionist was coming up the stairs. The books had been making a lot of noise so it had only been a matter of time before someone complained.

"What is going on in here?" The receptionist stopped a few feet away from the table, taking in the scene of destruction.

Suddenly another book flew by her, barely missing her head, and landed with a thud on the rest of the books covering the table. The receptionist's eyes widened. She didn't quite know what to think of this. Maybe she was hallucinating? That was the last time she would believe her roommate when he assured her that those mushrooms weren't dodgy.

She quietly turned around and went back down the stairs. She should check out a book on botany and memorise all the different kinds of mushrooms, just to avoid these moments – especially in the workplace. Talk about irresponsible.

Miss Level had no idea why the receptionist had just turned around and let them be, but it was for the best so she just shrugged and continued going through the books. "Maybe we should keep a few of these. They could probably help us as well."

"Is there an anti-locator spell in any of them?" Petulia snapped. "Because as soon as we find *The Big Book of Dale*, we need to un-jinx me. Damn it."

"Well, you are going to have to wait for a while because it's not here." Miss Level picked up the last book – a thick blue specimen – and tossed it on the pile of rejects.

"Are you sure?" Petulia poked her head out from under the table and was instantly hit in the face by one of the books that had been perched on top of it.

"Are you kidding me?" She raised her voice while she vigorously rubbed her nose. "It's not enough that they find me, they actually have to touch me as well? I can't bloody believe this." If there was ever an ounce of humour in Petulia, there was no trace of it any more.

"This is quickly remedied." Miss Level came over to the table and ducked underneath it, still afraid of getting smacked in the head as well. She then lifted her hand and blindly felt around for one of the books on the table. She grabbed it – the damn thing would not stop moving – and dragged it under the table. Then she swiftly tapped Petulia's arm with the book. It immediately stopped moving and twitching and dropped to the floor.

"Huh," was all Petulia could think of to say. She extended her arm towards Miss Level, who was already reaching up for another book. That one was also tapped against Petulia's arm and fell to the floor.

They continued doing this until the entire tabletop was empty. It didn't take too long. All the while Gabriel was watching them in amusement: two grown women sitting underneath a table, playing with books. It must have been quite a funny sight.

When they finished Petulia carefully came out of hiding. There didn't seem to be any more books heading towards her. She smiled hesitantly.

"All right. Let's go." Miss Level lifted her bag, and stuffed two books into it.

Petulia frowned. "What are you doing?"

"These two might come in handy one day." Miss Level swung her bag over her shoulder and started towards the stairs. Gabriel quickly followed her down.

Petulia looked around, then toed one of the books on the floor. No reaction.

"Ha!" Then she left as well.

A few blocks away from the library Adam and Shep had stopped walking. An elaborately decorated box, big enough for a person to sit in, was coming towards them. Well, it was actually being carried towards them. Four men were positioned at each corner of the box to carry the thing.

Adam stared at it. Well, not really at the box, more at the men carrying it. There was something strange about them. The closer they got, the more he could see what was so weird about them: one of them had scales, another one had a tail, the third had a beak, and the fourth…was that a third eye?

When the box finally reached them, a voice from inside yelled, "Stop!" and the men immediately halted. There was a door with a small window in the box. Adam watched in amazement as the curtain covering the window was slid to the side. A round face surrounded by a lot of tulle appeared. The face smiled at Adam. "Hello."

"Hello." Not knowing what else to do, Adam just replied. Somehow he knew that this was the smart thing to do when faced with this person in the box.

"I haven't seen you around before. Are you new to the city?"

"Yes, I just arrived today."

Shep barked, and Adam corrected himself.

"Well, *we* just arrived today." He patted Shep's head.

The face in the box looked at the dog with unsuccessfully veiled disgust. "That's nice." Then it turned back to Adam and smiled again. "Welcome to our fair city. I am Princess Clarice, but I'm sure you already knew that."

"No, I didn't, but it's nice to meet you." Adam held out his hand. He had seen people do this, and wanted to try it. Princess Clarice looked at it, not quite knowing what to do – nobody had ever shaken her hand before. Out of curiosity, she held out her hand as well. Adam immediately grabbed it – gently of course – and shook it. Both of them smiled at each other.

Princess Clarice's cheeks suddenly flushed. "Would you care to have dinner with me?" She couldn't believe she had just invited a strange man, whose name she didn't even know, to have dinner with her.

Adam regarded her for a while and then replied, "Sure. I'd love to." She wasn't really what he looked for in a meal and he was pretty sure that it would not be a good idea to eat her, but he figured he might try a normal meal and see how it went.

Shep was a little more cautious, and whined. Adam looked at him – still holding Princess Clarice's hand.

"Of course, I cannot come without my trusty companion."

At this Princess Clarice regarded the dog again. She didn't like it, but if the dog not coming was a deal-breaker for the gorgeous man in front of her, she would just have to cope with that. She smiled.

"Of course he can come."

Shep was happy and showed it the only way he knew how: he barked and jumped up and down. This, of course, startled Princess Clarice so much that she fell back inside the box.

"Easy, Shep." Adam patted his head and scratched behind his ears, which immediately calmed Shep down.

Hesitantly, Princess Clarice stuck her head out of the box again. "Uhm, well…why don't you come over to my place tonight? Eight o'clock all right for you?" She smiled again.

"That sounds good. The big pink palace, right?"

"That's right. I'll see you tonight, then." With those words she closed the curtain and yelled, "Go."

Just as the box was being carried around the corner, Adam sat down on his haunches next to Shep. "She seems like an important lady. Make sure I don't eat her, will you?"

Shep barked. He had already figured that one out for himself.

Eight

Change of Plans

"What shall we do now?" Petulia, Miss Level and Gabriel were standing in front of the library.

"We should probably try to find another way to locate *The Big Book of Dale*," Petulia suggested. Just at that moment a *Teen Witch* magazine flew right into her face, opened at an interview with God. Petulia peeled the magazine from her face. "Damn it. We really cannot escape this guy."

Miss Level took the magazine from her. "Why would he be in *Teen Witch*?" She frowned. "Isn't he too old?"

"It's probably because he started that school of magic of his."

Miss Level speed-read the article and had to agree with Petulia. God was going on and on about admission interviews and essays. "This is a very boring interview. No wonder the magazine is going under."

"Is it? I didn't know that." Petulia turned her head and saw Princess Clarice's box coming around the corner. "Damn it."

Miss Level looked up and saw the reason for Petulia's curse. "Bloody hell." She quickly glanced at Gabriel, who was standing next to her, and hissed at him, "Don't say a word. Don't sing either."

Gabriel frowned, but nodded to show that he understood. He looked at the box that had caused this sudden tension and noticed something off about it. First of all, it was being carried – most boxes he had seen around the city had wheels. Second, what was wrong with those men?

A voice yelled, "Stop!" and the four manlike creatures stopped in front of them. The curtain slid to the side and a face appeared. It wasn't until she spoke that Gabriel realised who this was.

"Miss Level. Petulia. Are you two finishing up my order?" Princess Clarice smiled at them and then looked at Gabriel. "Is this him?"

She looked him up and down and found everything to her liking – a good thing he was wearing a hat.

"Yes."

"No."

Petulia looked at Miss Level in confusion. She had started to suspect that Miss Level was developing feelings for Gabriel, but she had never thought that this would interfere with the business transaction that was the root of Gabriel's existence.

Miss Level thought it best not to look at Petulia. "This is not the man we had in mind for you. He is just helping us with some things." She glanced at Gabriel and could see how he was trying not to smile. "Kind of like a handyman."

"Oh." Princess Clarice's face immediately reflected her loathing. She didn't like handymen. Labourers were beneath her. She wanted a man who was well read, and smart, and charming, and blindingly handsome. She suddenly had a flashback to the man she had just met and she smiled, her eyes sparkling.

"Well, let me know how it goes. You still have two days left."

Princess Clarice decided it would be imprudent to tell the two witches about the man she had met. It was still early days. She would find out over dinner if the mystery man was 'the one'. She had a good feeling, though.

She suddenly realised she was still staring at the handyman, so she withdrew and closed the curtain. "Go."

Petulia, Miss Level and Gabriel watched the box disappear around the corner. Then Petulia looked at Miss Level, decided there would be no benefit in arguing with her, snorted and walked away.

At the sound of the snort, Miss Level and Gabriel turned around. Miss Level sighed and followed Petulia. She had no idea how to explain what had just happened. She was still trying to figure it out herself. But it didn't seem like Petulia actually wanted to talk – she just walked on with big strides. Miss Level grabbed Gabriel's hand and they walked on as well.

A horrifying screech was heard throughout the city. Even Gerald, the old guard out front, heard it and knew something was terribly wrong.

A young waitress named Mary came rushing out of one of the finer establishments of the city. She had her hands in her hair and was crying and screaming all over the place. Several people came out of their houses. Others stopped walking and joined the small crowd that was forming in front of The Last Call. A young man stepped forward and grabbed Mary's shoulders.

"What happened?" He held her fast, but she wouldn't stop shaking and crying. The screaming had stopped, though. The young man decided he wouldn't be able to get any coherent answer out of her in this state. He held her tight and rubbed his hands over her back, trying to calm her down.

The young man's brother stepped up to him. "I'll take a look inside. See if anything is wrong." With those words the brother disappeared into the tavern.

Mary immediately started to sob loudly and grabbed hold of the young man. She didn't want to think about what she had seen inside, but she couldn't get that image out of her head. Just then the brother came running out, as white as a ghost. He ran straight into Mary and the young man, trying to escape the sight he had just seen. The people in the crowd surrounding them were curious as to what was going on.

"What happened, Peter?" The young man, still rubbing Mary's back, was torn between comforting her and calming down his younger brother. When it didn't look like the young woman was about to let go of him, he tried to calm his brother by talking in a soothing voice. "Peter, it's all right. Just tell me what's wrong and I will make it all better."

Peter shook his head, face pale, and spoke, teeth chattering. "There is nothing you can do, Paul." He shook his head again, tears in his eyes. "It's just horrible..." His voice faded away.

Now Paul was not a fearful person, but neither was his brother. So Paul was not too keen on going inside that tavern. He knew, however, that out of all the people standing there, he would be the best choice to go in. He gave the girl in his arms a small squeeze; then he motioned to an older woman to take her from him. The woman immediately realised why he wanted this, and gently took over comforting Mary.

Paul straightened his shirt and walked through the door of the tavern. At first glance everything seemed normal, even though the establishment was completely empty. He looked around, taking in every inch of the room, frowning when nothing seemed out of place, except maybe a glass of ale that was left half empty on one of the tables in the corner.

Then he noticed that the door to the kitchen was halfway open. He neared it and pushed it open fully. He could see the entire kitchen now, though he didn't have to. He immediately saw what had made the others run, right in the middle of the counter. Bloody bones, with a few bits of meat still on them, but the most disturbing thing about the spectacle was probably the apron, cast aside on top of a pile of bloody clothes. There was still some blood dripping off the counter. Reluctantly, his eyes followed the drip. That's when he saw part of a leg and involuntarily lost his lunch on the spot.

Following Petulia around when she was in one of her moods was Miss Level's least favourite pastime. Unhappily, she did so anyway.

Suddenly they all heard the horrifying screech. All three of them turned around at the same time. When they didn't see anyone rushing towards them, they looked at each other and decided to just keep walking the way they had been heading. Although they still had no idea where they were actually going.

*

Adam and Shep also heard the horrifying screech. Adam had a vague feeling that this might have something to do with the owner of the tavern. Shep, however, sniffed the air and smelled only fear and horror. He was extremely certain that this had everything to do with the owner of the tavern. He barked at Adam.

"You're right. Let's keep going." Adam looked from left to right, as if in confusion. "Which way do you think we should go?"

As far away from the tavern as possible, Shep thought. He barked again and turned left.

Petulia had had enough. "You know what?"

Miss Level was so surprised that Petulia had broken the silence that she was at a loss for words. "Huh?"

"I don't think it's wise to fall for one of your own creations." Petulia had stopped in the middle of the street and was standing with her hands on her hips, glaring at Miss Level. "Do you?"

"What do you mean, 'falling for'?" Miss Level hadn't quite accepted yet that she was falling for Gabriel. She liked him, yes, but surely it was nothing more than that. Right?

"I understand. He's handsome, in spite of the horns, but he is still a job. And you go and tell Princess Clarice that he's the handyman?" Petulia's voice kept rising. "What were you thinking?"

"Well…"

"You do realise that we have to find another man now. Don't you?"

"Well…"

"Oh, forget it." Petulia vaguely waved her hands towards Miss Level while she turned around and started to walk away again.

"Well…" Miss Level was stunned.

Gabriel decided that the command to not say or sing anything was not in effect any more, so he opened his mouth and took hold of Miss Level's hands.

"I know that we have just met, but I can't get you out of my head. I don't know what to do. Do you feel the same way too?"

Miss Level could do nothing else but stare at this gorgeous man, and his gorgeous mouth, and suddenly she wondered what it would be like to kiss him. She closed her eyes and shook her head. She was getting too old for this. And she had never done this before – she had never been in love and didn't know what to expect or what to do. And then there was this handsome young man – created only two days ago – who already knew more than she did and who was letting her know that he was in love with her. Was he serious? How could he possibly know that?

She withdrew her hands from his and went after Petulia. She needed to focus on something else. She would deal with this later.

Gabriel was confused. Had he done it wrong? No. Had he mistaken the signs Miss Level had been giving him? He didn't think so. Maybe he had. Maybe she thought he was just a stupid boy who needed protection. Well, he didn't. He was smart and big enough – even if he wasn't old enough – to do whatever he wanted to. And he was going to follow them, and protect them. Ha, that would show her. He stomped his feet and went after the women.

*

"Do you think I need new clothes?" Adam looked at his pinstriped three-piece suit. He wanted to think about something other than the screech they had heard and the consequences said screech might have for him. So he decided to focus on the date. At least he thought it was a date.

Shep barked once. By that time Adam had figured out that one bark meant 'yes', two barks meant 'no' and a lot of barks meant 'Are you freaking kidding me?'

"We will stop at the next clothes shop."

They strolled down the street, passing at least three clothes shops. But every time Adam had one reason or another not to enter the store: only women's clothing, only pregnant women's clothing, only children's clothing, only fishermen's clothing. Shep was getting fretful. He was only seconds away from a lot of barks.

Suddenly Adam stopped and looked through the window of yet another shop. Hope grew within Shep, and when Adam actually went in, he was as giddy as a newborn lamb – at least I think a newborn lamb is giddy. But when Shep entered and saw the obese woman behind the counter, he decided to bring out the 'Are you freaking kidding me?' barks. Adam paid him no attention and walked up to the counter.

The woman behind the counter looked up and smiled when she saw the handsome young man enter her little shop. "Welcome." She put away the magazine she was reading. "Are you looking for something special?"

Adam smiled back. "Actually, I am. I have a date tonight but I really don't have anything to wear."

Although she was a little disappointed that the handsome man already had a date, the woman decided a little innocent flirting wouldn't be so bad.

"You look great in what you're wearing now."

Adam looked down. "Yes, I know, but she has already seen me in this." He looked up with a serious face. "Wouldn't that give the wrong impression?"

Surprised that a man would actually think about that, the woman put her hand to her chest.

"Wow. That is just amazing." She quickly recovered and came out from behind the counter. She walked to one of the clothes racks and selected a stylish pair of trousers. Then she went to another rack and picked up a shirt. Last but not least, she went to the shelves against the wall and grabbed one of the waistcoats.

She turned towards Adam, smiling. "I am sure you look great in anything you put on, but please, try these." She handed over the clothes and showed Adam where the changing rooms were. He stepped into one and closed the curtain behind him.

Shep, who had decided to keep an eye on everything, stood guard in front of the curtain. He could hear Adam taking off his clothes and changing into the new ones.

The woman had returned to the counter and was pretending to read her magazine again, but her eyes kept sliding over to the closed curtains. "Do you need any help?"

A muffled, "No thank you," came from behind the curtain.

When Adam had put on the new clothes, he called Shep into the dressing room. Shep stuck his head underneath the curtain and looked up at Adam, who was twisting his body to try and see his backside in the mirror. Adam suddenly stopped twisting and turning and gazed undecidedly at his reflection.

He looked down. "What do you think, Shep?"

Shep cocked his head, looked Adam up and down and then barked once.

"Are you sure?" Adam twisted around again to look at his bottom.

Shep barked again.

"Well, all right."

Adam started to take off the clothes again, so Shep wiggled backwards from under the curtain. When he turned around, he noticed the woman staring at him quizzically. About two minutes later Adam reappeared and took the new clothes to the counter.

The woman took them from him. "Is there anything else?"

"Just a bag will be fine." Adam watched the woman tally up the prices.

"That's 85.30 Edmunds, thanks." The woman started putting the clothes into a bag, when she noticed the handsome man wasn't getting his wallet out. "85.30, please," she repeated.

Adam just looked at her, wondering what she was going on about. All of a sudden he realised that she probably wanted something in return. He started patting his pockets, but came up with nothing so smiled apologetically.

"I am so sorry, but I don't know what to do."

The woman hesitated. She decided that he hadn't gone on his date yet, so she might as well have some fun with him.

"Well, I know something you can do."

She walked over to the door and locked it. Then she drew the curtains and crossed the shop, back to where Adam was standing.

Shep knew what Adam was thinking at that moment: nobody can see us. Adam licked his lips, thinking he probably shouldn't. Before he could do or say anything, the woman threw her arms around his neck and kissed him passionately.

Adam had no idea what was happening but decided to go with the flow.

Shep had not seen that one coming. He lay down and watched the show.

By the time Miss Level caught up with her, Petulia had come up with a new idea. Being smacked in the head by so many magic books and magazines had done something good. She figured that *The Big Book of Dale* would come to her. Seeing that every other magic book in the vicinity was drawn to her anyway, *The Big Book of Dale* couldn't be that far off. All she had to do was wait for it.

Of course, the city would not be an excellent place to do this – people were already looking at her funny because of the magazines flying out of newspaper stands and landing on her face. Maybe they could make up a spell to prevent the same issue of a magazine from showing up over and over again – she had already seen the current edition of *Teen Witch* seven times. It was annoying, and the interview with God wasn't getting any better. But first things first.

Miss Level was surprised when Petulia suddenly entered a shop. She hesitated, and decided to wait outside for her to return. If Petulia needed help or anything, she would have asked, right? She couldn't be that mad.

Gabriel stood next to Miss Level. He didn't know why she had stopped or what she was waiting for – he hadn't seen Petulia enter the shop as he had only just rounded the corner. But he figured she would tell him if she wanted to. He had done his part; it was up to her now.

An early printing of *Witchcraft for Dummies* flew past them, through the open door and into the store. Surprisingly enough, it was not followed by a 'Damn it' as expected.

Petulia came out of the store carrying a giant black umbrella. "That should solve the immediate problem for now."

She nodded at her two companions and then gestured for them to follow her, which they did. Always follow the man with the plan – or in this case the woman.

Adam stumbled out of the clothes shop. He felt strangely satisfied, and was smiling. He hadn't known he could feel like this as a result of something other than eating. The woman came to the door and blew him a kiss. Then she returned to the counter, leaving the door wide open.

Shep exited the shop as well. He was happy that the woman was still around, but was also slightly disturbed by what he had seen. At least he felt some hope that the date that night might not go as badly as he first expected. He barked once at Adam and then pulled at his waistcoat. Adam was still smiling stupidly, gazing at a spot in front of him but not really seeing anything. Shep licked his hand, which caused him to snap out of it, still smiling like an idiot though.

"Did you see that, Shep? I didn't eat her."

Shep barked once.

"I like this new thing. Do you think I can do that again tonight?"

Shep thought about that for a minute. He barked twice.

"Why not?" Adam frowned. "That was fun." Then he seemed to remember that the woman had locked the door before jumping him. It probably wasn't something you could just *do* to people. Adam shrugged. He would see how things went tonight. Maybe he could tell Princess Clarice that it was either that or getting eaten. Hmm, probably not such a good idea.

Shep was standing a bit further ahead, barking at him. Adam walked to the corner where he was standing and followed him to wherever he was going. Not having to decide what to do right then made it easier to think about what to do later that night.

Nine

Let's Wait and See…

It took a while but eventually Miss Level figured out that Petulia was heading for the closest gate out of the city. She still had no idea what she was planning, but she was also curious about this side of the wall. She had never gone through that gate and wondered what they would find.

Coincidentally, Petulia didn't know what to expect either; she just wanted to get out of the city as fast as she could. The umbrella helped a great deal against the onslaught of books and magazines but she was fairly certain it wouldn't hold out for that much longer. She would figure something out when they got out of the city.

When they neared the gate, it looked rusted as hell. All three of them stopped in front of it and stared. Petulia shrugged and decided to give it a push and see what happened. Nothing.

Miss Level and Gabriel decided to help. Nothing.

After pushing at the rusted iron gate for about ten minutes, Petulia looked around and noticed a chain hanging down beside it. Figuring it couldn't do any harm, she pulled it. A loud clang resounded. They ducked and covered their ears. Dust fell down upon their heads.

When the ringing in their ears was finally reduced to a gentle hum, a man opened a small peephole in the gate. They could only see one of his eyes as he looked them over. Then he shifted so his mouth was in front of the hole.

"What do you want?" he yelled, and then turned his head so his ear was pointed in their direction.

After a quick glance at the others, Petulia stepped forward. "WE WANT TO GET OUT."

The man behind the gate pulled back. "You don't have to yell."

Petulia didn't think she was yelling, but couldn't be quite sure as the humming in her head was still going on. "I'M SORRY."

The man figured he might as well step back a little if the funny-looking woman with the umbrella was going to keep yelling at him. Of course this meant he would have to yell back at her.

"WHY DO YOU WANT TO LEAVE?"

"WE WERE JUST VISITING AND WANT TO GO HOME NOW."

The man narrowed his eyes at her. "DOES THIS HAVE ANYTHING TO DO WITH THAT HORRIBLE SCREAM EARLIER? DO THE THREE OF YOU KNOW MORE ABOUT THAT?"

To be honest, Petulia had already forgotten about that, being so caught up in her own problems. "WE HAVE NO IDEA WHAT THAT WAS ABOUT, BUT HONESTLY, WHO WOULD WANT

TO STAY IN A CITY WITH SUCH SCREAMS?"

The guard had to agree with her. When he heard the screech himself, he was very happy to be outside the wall. "IF YOU SWEAR TO PRINCESS CLARICE THAT YOU HAD NOTHING TO DO WITH IT, I'LL LET YOU OUT."

For people living in or close to the city, swearing to Princess Clarice was as official an oath as one could possibly make. Petulia nodded to Miss Level and Gabriel. All three of them were fairly certain they had nothing to do with the scream, so they sang, "*I swear*," to try and mask the fact that Gabriel couldn't talk normally.

The guard thought it was a bit weird, but an oath was an oath so he slapped the peephole closed and started turning the wheels to open the gate. The iron, but mostly the rust, gave a lot of resistance. The gate had clearly not been opened in a long, long time. When it finally gave way, the gate scraped over the dirt road. It opened far enough for the three of them to walk through.

The guard was hanging over the mechanism, completely exhausted. He gave them a weak smile.

"I've always wondered what would happen," he continued, between gasping breaths. "My great-grandfather was the original guard of this gate. Then it was my grandfather's turn, and then my father's. And now it's just me." He gazed up at the gate, while the three travellers politely waited for him to finish. "I don't think any of them ever saw the gate open." His gaze dropped back to the mechanism. "Oh, well." He grasped the wheel and started turning it again. The gate slowly closed.

Petulia didn't want to wait for the gate to be completely

closed. She figured the guard had been too busy to notice the flying books, but he wouldn't be busy for too much longer. So she motioned for Miss Level and Gabriel to quietly follow her.

When the gate was finally closed, the guard turned around.

"How rude."

He slid to the floor and decided to rest for a while before going home and telling his wife what had happened today. For once he would have a different story to tell when she asked how his day had been. He smiled.

Shep was leading Adam, but he didn't really know where to. When they crossed a bridge, he put his head under the railing and looked beneath it. He pulled back and barked at Adam, who was still dazed from his earlier experience. If a dog were able to shrug, Shep would have done so at that exact moment. Instead he looked at Adam for a few seconds and then pulled his waistcoat to signal to him to follow.

After they crossed the bridge, Shep immediately turned right and walked down the embankment. Not knowing what else to do, Adam just followed. Underneath the bridge was a small patch of grass with a few rocks. Shep laid himself down and barked at Adam. Adam in turn looked around, noted that this was as good a place as any to collect his thoughts and sat on one of the rocks. He put his elbows on his knees and his head in his hands and stared into the water.

Shep looked at Adam, decided he wasn't going anywhere and put his head on his paws to rest a bit. He would have to be alert when his master went on his date.

Suddenly he heard heavy, thudding footsteps on the bridge above them. Somehow he knew this had something to do with the scream and the tavern owner. This was going to come back and bite them in the ass. Currently, however, there was nothing to be done about it so he shut his eyes and went to sleep, leaving Adam to his musings.

Petulia had started to figure out that this day just kept getting worse and worse. She should have guessed as much in the morning when she saw Gabriel in the kitchen, rinsing the blueberries. She should have stopped him and taken over. Maybe all this could have been prevented. Maybe that would have stopped Miss Level from developing this stupid crush, and she would not have cast the stupid spell on *The Big Book of Dale*. She glanced over her shoulder at the two lovebirds and was immediately struck in the face by another *Teen Witch*.

"Damn it." Her mood would not be lifting soon.

Miss Level and Gabriel were following Petulia to wherever she was going. Miss Level was still not sure how she should act towards Gabriel. She really liked him, but wasn't this the definition of 'robbing the cradle'? He was so darn young and she was so darn old. How in the world could this ever work out?

Gabriel was walking closely behind Miss Level. He had no idea what his next move should be, so he decided to just enjoy being close to her. Currently he was watching her rather curvy backside swishing from side to side. He felt a strange stirring below. The sensation made him light-headed and he stumbled, bumping into Miss Level – he was following her very closely.

Miss Level turned around. "Are you all right?"

A little confused, Gabriel just nodded and stared into her eyes. The only thing she could do was stare back. On impulse, Gabriel started to lower his head. This made Miss Level snap out of it. She blushed, coughed and turned back around, happy to see Petulia hadn't noticed a thing. She quickly joined her, leaving Gabriel alone with his stirrings.

Back in the city, the crowd in front of The Last Call had grown exponentially. The young waitress, Mary, and the two young men, Peter and Paul, were sitting outside on the pavement. All three of them were very shaken up.

Only a few minutes ago the city guard had shown up. The unmistakable thudding footsteps had resounded across the entire city and people had naturally followed them to find out what was going on. The city guard were used to this and had closed off a perimeter around the tavern so they could work in peace.

Chief Vernon Hightower – whose name most definitely did not match his appearance – had not yet entered the tavern, and had ordered the other guards to wait until he was certain of what they could expect. So he faced the three pale youngsters and wondered which approach would be best to get the information he needed.

The girl was sitting between the men, but was leaning towards the elder of them. The younger man kept throwing glances at the elder, so Chief Hightower figured he would be the one to talk to first.

"I am Chief Hightower. What is your name?" He went down

on his haunches so he could look the young man in the eye without seeming too controlling. Of course, even standing he would have had the same effect, but he was the kind of man who would always try to put people as much at ease as possible. This made him an excellent chief of the city guard, because people tended to trust him. They never expected anything bad from him, which had led to many criminals' downfall.

"Paul." The young man looked at the chief and tried to be as brave as possible. He didn't want the other two to find out that he was as scared as he could be.

"Hello, Paul." Chief Hightower gave him a small, polite smile. "I wish we could have met under other circumstances. However, being that this is not the case, I do have a few questions for you. Are you up for it?" He looked at him expectantly.

Paul just nodded. He figured he could just tell the chief everything he knew and saw and then he could go home. He wanted this entire day to be over as quickly as possible.

"All right. Why don't you tell me what happened? Start from the beginning."

Whatever Chief Hightower had been expecting, it wasn't what Paul told him. He had never heard of a man being eaten. Lamb, yes. Cow, yes. Even, on occasion, a horse. But a full-grown man? That was definitely a first. The chief resisted the urge to go inside – surely this young man was playing tricks on him? – and focused on what Paul was saying.

"And then I threw up." Paul felt deeply ashamed, and threw a furtive look at the chief. He wasn't sure why but he really didn't want to upset or anger this man. "I'm sorry I ruined your crime scene." He bowed his head in shame.

Chief Hightower put his hand on the young man's shoulder. "I'm sure you haven't ruined anything. I will go inside now and take a look around. Thank you for your help."

"Does this mean we can go home?"

"Yes. We have your contact information should we need anything else."

With those words, Chief Hightower stood up. The three youngsters followed his example and left.

The chief took a deep breath and called his second over to him. "Inspector Small?"

It took a while before his second reacted, but when he did, everyone around knew it. The oversized inspector had also been dealt the wrong name. Of course, in his family he was actually the smallest, so it made sense in a way. He made his way towards the chief.

"We are going in," was all the chief said before he walked through the door. The inspector ducked down and followed. He immediately bumped into Chief Hightower, who had stopped right inside the door and was taking in the scene.

"It seems normal enough." The chief let his eyes pass over every surface, and stopped when he noticed the half-full glass of ale. He cocked his head. "We should take that with us."

Inspector Small grabbed a notebook from his pocket and wrote it down. After that, they slowly walked through the room, scanning the entire place, heading towards the kitchen. They didn't see anything else out of place so they turned their attention to the next room.

Both men paled when they saw the counter. They had seen some gruesome deaths in their line of work but nothing had quite prepared them for this. The chief immediately knew how Paul had felt when he had stood in the same spot, and fought hard to keep his own lunch down. His training helped, of course.

"Well, it seems we have our first murder by famine." Chief Hightower swallowed. "There doesn't seem to be a lot we can do here right now. Let's get the techies in here. We'll wait for their report." He pivoted and marched outside.

Inspector Small was still a bit dazed but let his eyes take in every detail anyway. This was a horrible crime and he didn't want to miss anything that might help them catch the fiend. After a few moments he had to agree that they should let the techies do their stuff. He turned around as well and went to give them their instructions, thankful that he didn't have their job.

Ten

Love is in the Air…

After they had been walking for a while Miss Level asked, "Where are you going? If we keep walking this way, we'll get to Heaven City soon."

Petulia said over her shoulder, "We won't go that far. There is a meadow up ahead if I'm not mistaken."

Miss Level wasn't so sure but she had never come this way before, so she just shrugged and followed, with Gabriel in tow.

They passed a small farm. The petite building was a bit crooked with age but the garden had been well tended. There was a hand-painted sign outside that read: *Fresh Vegetables For Sale*. The writing was a bit askew, but the sign was very proper and inviting. Petulia figured they would need something to eat later on, so she opened the little gate and walked through the garden. Miss Level, who had always liked fresh vegetables, followed.

When the three of them reached the front door, Petulia raised her hand and knocked. They could hear a pot crashing to the ground and then a lot of swearing. Tiny feet shuffled to the door. It opened slightly, revealing a small head, glowering at the visitors.

"What do you want?" it snapped.

"Well, we were thinking of buying some vegetables, but if this is the service we are going to receive, I think we will just turn around and be on our merry way." Petulia turned to go. She'd had a lousy day and was not going to be snapped at by a dwarf.

"No, no, no. That won't do." The door opened wider and a small female head, very similar to the one that had opened the door, appeared. This one was smiling brightly. "Please, please, come in." She waved her hands in a welcoming, come-hither kind of way.

Petulia, Miss Level and Gabriel ducked inside. The male dwarf grumbled and closed the door behind them while the female showed them to the table. She immediately grabbed the fallen pot from off the tabletop and cleared the spilt vegetables.

"Did you see my sign outside? Is that what made you come in?"

"Yes," Petulia said hesitantly.

The female dwarf elbowed the male one. "See, I told you it would work." Still smiling brightly, she faced Petulia again. "So what would you like?"

"What have you got? 'Vegetables' is not really very specific, is it?"

"Oh." Not offended at all. "We've got carrots, squash, cauliflower, potatoes, green beans, lettuce, tomato – which is technically not a vegetable, but still – peas, broccoli, radish, pumpkin, cabbage, cucumber and spinach. We have got fruit as well. Would you like to hear that list too?"

Petulia, Miss Level and Gabriel were a bit taken aback, so they just nodded.

"We have got apricots, apples, pears, pineapples, limes, lemons, melons, strawberries, blackberries, blueberries, raspberries, oranges, and loads of other stuff. Would you like to see the orchards?"

"Uhm, no thank you." Petulia glanced at her companions to make sure they weren't going to say or do anything stupid. But both of them seemed to be caught up in their own little world. "We will take some tomatoes and lettuce. A few carrots, potatoes and cucumbers. And an assortment of berries if that's all right."

"Oh, yes. Yes, it is." The female beamed. She turned to the sulking man and sent him to get everything. While he was gone, she tallied everything up and presented Petulia with the bill.

Petulia was surprised that it was such a small amount. She made a mental note to always shop at small farms from now on. The male dwarf came back with a basket filled with natural goodies and handed it over to her. She thanked them and gestured to Miss Level and Gabriel to get up and go.

When they opened the door, a voluminous book almost knocked Petulia and her basket to the ground. Fortunately she was able to duck in time. Unfortunately, the male dwarf wasn't. The woman quickly said her goodbyes and closed the door.

Petulia noticed all the magic books lying in front of the door, squiggling about. She hastily opened her umbrella, then squatted down and patted every one of them to make them stop squirming. After that she got back up and walked away from the tiny farm, with her unusually silent companions.

*

Shep opened his eyes and immediately realised that something was very wrong: Adam was nowhere to be seen. He sprang to his paws and started turning around and around, yapping a bit. Where would Adam have gone to? Why had he closed his eyes? He knew he had to pay extra attention to this master. Not out of fear of what he might do to him, but of what he might do to others.

He sniffed the air, trying to pick up Adam's scent. That was going to be very difficult in a city like this, but he would sniff like he had never sniffed before. He put his nose to the ground and started to sniff his way up the embankment.

There! There it was! His master's scent! He quickly ran in the same direction as his master had done not too long ago. In the same direction as those thudding footsteps had gone about an hour before that.

Miss Level had made a decision. While they were in the small cottage with the dwarves, she had been watching Gabriel, covertly of course. He had made no eye contact with her, and had made no unwanted approaches or signals. There were a couple of reasons she could think of for this. One: seeing that his previous efforts had been to no avail, he had given up. Somehow Miss Level thought this was not Gabriel's way. Two: he was giving her space to think about everything. This was very considerate of him. She decided to believe this reason, and started to think about everything.

Gabriel had been listening intently to the conversation between Petulia and the small female person in the cottage. He was trying to keep the stirrings below to a minimum and had quickly realised that looking at Miss Level had the exact opposite effect. He was now gazing at everything around him, as long as it wasn't Miss Level.

Suddenly his eye fell on Petulia. She was a weird woman, very bossy. He did not like her very much. Of course, getting hit in the head occasionally by flying books would be enough to ruin anybody's mood. He vaguely realised that thinking about Petulia had the desired effect on his nether regions, so he continued doing just that.

Shep had been running for a few minutes when he came upon a crowd of people. He saw Adam standing near them, trying to listen to what people were talking about. Shep looked around and quickly figured out that they had been here before and that it hadn't turned out very well the last time. Well, not for the fat tavern owner anyway. He quietly crept towards Adam, picking up hints of conversation along the way.

"Has there been a robbery?"

"I heard that Mike had tried to set his tavern on fire for insurance reasons."

"Looks like it didn't work, 'cause the city guard are looking very serious. I don't see any smoke either."

A bit further on, the people were getting closer to the truth.

"Where is Mike anyway?"

"I think he's still in there."

"What do you mean?"

"Think about it. Mike is the most awful person I know.

I can't understand why Mary keeps working for him. But he loves that tavern. It's his life. If anything were going on with it, he would be here."

"You're right." Both men turned back towards the tavern, wide-eyed.

When Shep reached Adam, he gently tugged on his sleeve. Adam looked down. He seemed a bit confused.

"Why are all these people here, Shep?"

The man standing in front of him turned around. "Something horrible happened in The Last Call. Mary came out screaming her head off a few hours ago." The man looked Adam up and down. "Say, do I know you? You look a bit familiar." He shook his head. "Anyway, I had been in there about an hour before it happened. Didn't see anything funny. Just the usual crowd, having lunch."

He cocked his head. "I am sure I have seen you before." Then he turned back to the tavern, while still talking to Adam and Shep. "I don't know what's happened but it can't be good. Not with the city guard here. Whatever it is, they'll figure it out. They always do." By then he had forgotten whom he had been talking to, but when he turned back around, there was nobody there. He shrugged and continued watching the events in front of him.

Shep was dragging Adam by his sleeve until they rounded the corner.

"Am I in trouble, Shep?"

One bark.

"Do you think I can fix this?"

Two barks.

"You're probably right." Adam straightened his tie, which

113

wasn't really necessary. "It's too late now anyway. I should probably just focus on tonight." His hands stilled on his tie. "I can still go on my date, can't I?"

Shep thought that wasn't such a good idea. So he barked twice, glanced at Adam and pulled his sleeve again. They should probably leave the city. But how was he going to get Adam to cancel his date and leave? They headed back to the bridge for some more thinking time.

After they had been walking for a while Petulia stopped at a wide,-open space, occupied only by grass and an occasional shrub. She nodded and stepped off the path they had been following, made her way to the centre of the meadow and looked around. A smooth rock seemed to be waiting just for her, so she walked over to it and sat down. She put the basket next to her, but kept the umbrella tightly in her hand.

Miss Level and Gabriel had been watching all this from the safety of the path. When they realised nothing else was going to happen, they decided to join Petulia.

"It took the two of you long enough." Petulia gestured for them to sit down as well.

"So what's the plan?" Miss Level was curious as to why they were sitting in the centre of a meadow.

"I figured" – book – "that sitting in" – book – "an open space" – book – "being assaulted by" – book – "books might" – book – "attract less attention" – book – "than doing the" – book – "same thing in a busy city." The seven books that had hit the umbrella during that one sentence were lying on the ground quivering.

Petulia casually reached down and ran her hand over each and every one of them.

Miss Level thought about it and had to agree that it made a lot of sense. Three more books flew into the umbrella.

"This umbrella" – book – "might not last" – book – "through the night," – book – "though."

Miss Level sat up straighter. "We could try to pitch a tent."

At this, Petulia regarded her quizzically. "And how would we do this?" Another book.

Miss Level looked defiantly at Petulia. "I can do a simple tent-resurrection spell. It's not that hard."

"Fine" – book – "but do it over there." Petulia waved her hand to the right side of the meadow. Unfortunately the hand was then not underneath the umbrella, and was immediately smacked by a hardback copy of *The Elemental Encyclopaedia of Witchcraft*. "Damn it."

Sensing a bout of curses coming on, Miss Level hastily got up and walked to the right side of the meadow. She stood stock-still with her hands hanging loosely at her sides and her eyes closed. She took a deep breath and mumbled a few words in Latin, while slowly raising her hands. As she did so, a slight purple glow emanated from her. The grass around her started to move. A circle with a radius of about ten feet appeared. The grass started to weave itself together to form a circular tent. As Miss Level raised her hands higher, the grass tent wove together tighter and higher. When her hands finally met above her head, the tent top knitted together and formed a roof. It was very impressive to see.

Gabriel, who had been watching the whole thing from his spot next to Petulia, had been amazed until he realised that Miss Level had disappeared inside the grass construction. He immediately stood up and walked around the tent to find a way in.

Inside, Miss Level was still in the centre of the tent with her eyes closed and her hands meeting above her head. She slowly lowered her hands and pointed in front of her, mumbling several other Latin words. She lowered her hands further, still pointing at the side of the tent. A zipper appeared.

Outside, Gabriel saw the zipper come into being and immediately walked over to it to open the side of the tent. Miss Level, who still had her eyes closed, was surprised to hear the zipper open, and was even more surprised to open her eyes and find Gabriel in the tent with her. He was just looking at her. All she could do was blush.

Gabriel stared at Miss Level in amazement. She was still giving off a faint purple glow that was sexy as hell. The shy blush wasn't helping either. He quietly turned around and closed the zipper. Then he turned back to Miss Level and strolled towards her, softly singing.

"I want to gently hold you, and bask in your glow. I know I already told you, but I need you to know. I tried to ignore this, but it just doesn't work. Right now, if we don't kiss, I might just go berserk."

Miss Level's knees were just about to give out, when Gabriel reached her and softly brushed her hair aside. She was completely helpless, as his head dipped lower and his lips found hers.

Petulia, who was still sitting outside, under the cover of her umbrella, quickly realised what was going on.

"That's just perfect. Don't mind me. I'll just wait here and continue being assaulted by heavy volumes of witchcraft encyclopaedias."

At the same moment, one of those volumes tore through her umbrella and smacked her right in the back of her head.

"Damn it."

Adam had been watching Shep lying close to the water. He wasn't sure what he was thinking about – wasn't even sure if Shep could think – but he figured it was about time he left for his date. He got up and saw Shep immediately rise as well.

"I should go if I am to meet the pink lady on time." He brushed the dirt off his clothes, straightened everything he could possibly straighten and started to leave.

Shep wasn't happy that Adam still wanted to go through with this date, but he followed him closely to make sure he couldn't get into any more trouble. But honestly, it couldn't get much worse, could it?

They walked up the slope and headed down the street towards the bright pink castle. Adam wasn't sure what he was going to do on this date but he had decided, based on recent developments, that he would not eat Princess Clarice. He just hoped she had other food available.

It didn't take them too long to reach the castle. They stopped in front of it and gazed up.

"It really is an ugly thing, isn't it?"

Shep just barked once.

Adam shrugged and walked over to the heavy-looking door.

There was a rope hanging next to it. Not really knowing what else to do, he pulled the rope. A loud bell chimed inside.

A few minutes later, a voice resounded from inside. "Who is it?"

"Uhm...Adam." He hesitantly looked at Shep, who just nodded. "Princess Clarice is expecting me."

"Ah, yes." They could hear several locks being unlocked on the inside. Finally the door opened and a rather small soldier appeared. "Her date." He looked Adam up and down, then stepped aside to let them in.

After they entered, the short soldier closed the door and turned around. "Follow me." He headed down a corridor.

They passed several doors and a lot of paintings, mainly depicting Princess Clarice herself, until they finally entered a gigantic dining room. A long, fully decked table was in the middle of the room. Adam had never seen so much crystal in one room. The old lady he had met on his first day had had a lot of crystal as well, but nothing compared to this. The silverware was also astonishing, and very, very shiny.

Princess Clarice was already sitting at the head of the table. Adam walked over to her and extended his hand again. It had gone well the first time, so he might as well stick to what he knew had worked before. Princess Clarice gently put her hand in his and gave him a shy smile. On impulse Adam bent down and kissed the tiny hand. Judging by the blush on Princess Clarice's cheeks and her smile growing bigger, he realised he had done something right. Maybe this dating business wasn't that hard after all.

Princess Clarice withdrew her hand and gestured to the other end of the table. Unfortunately Adam didn't understand what she meant by this weird waving gesture, but he figured she wanted him to sit down. So he grabbed the chair on the corner next to her and sat down.

Wide-eyed, Princess Clarice watched him. She was completely shocked. No one had ever done this. She wasn't sure what to do now. Asking him to get up and plant his gorgeous behind all the way at the other side of the table seemed like the worst idea in centuries.

She gave a small, nervous cough. Then she lifted a tiny bell and rang it. Immediately a door on the right side of the dining room, which had been hidden until then, opened and a man with an elephantine trunk appeared. Adam startled and watched how the man carried two bowls in his hands and a soup terrine with his trunk.

Princess Clarice followed his gaze. She had grown accustomed to seeing the unfortunate men who had been created by Petulia and Miss Level. She probably should have fired the old witches and gone to the Briar sisters, but she had gotten some first-class servants out of the deal and hadn't had to pay for them. Plus, Petulia and Miss Level had assured her that their latest creation was the best ever, so she had no worries. She glanced at Adam sitting at her table. No worries at all...

The man with the trunk handled the soup expertly and left right after serving. Adam felt suspicious of the soup, fairly certain that it would not be able to settle his stomach. But he had promised himself that he would give it a try, so he watched how Princess Clarice took the spoon, dragged it through the soup and lifted it to her mouth. He followed her example and was surprised at the exquisite taste of the watery food. He cleaned his bowl with a small piece of bread, conveniently located beside it. When he was finished Princess Clarice rang the little bell again, which made the trunk man come out and clear the table.

"So, Adam. How do you like our fair city?"

"Well, it's nice but smells kind of weird."

At the sight of Princess Clarice's face he realised this was not the response she had expected.

"But it smells nice in here."

Shep, who had been under the table since they had entered the room, buried his head under his paws and realised it was going to be a very long night.

Princess Clarice smiled awkwardly and rang the tiny bell again. This time a man with cloven hooves for feet appeared, balancing a couple of plates and a serving dish on his rather muscular arms. After he set everything on the table he vanished again, but quickly returned with a platter filled with neatly arranged steamed fish and vegetables. He put the platter on the table between Princess Clarice and Adam and lifted the top of the serving dish, exposing fragrant rice. Then he left the two of them alone. Adam again watched how Princess Clarice tackled this dish and followed her example.

Princess Clarice had quickly figured out that this date was going nowhere, and she was glad that she hadn't told Petulia and Miss Level about it. It was a shame, though, because this man really was a stunner. This was one of the reasons that she had commissioned the witches to make her a man anyway. Clearly there was a fault in the way men were constructed: they were either gorgeous but stupid or rude, or they were smart and polite but ugly as hell. Princess Clarice decided to endure this date and started to look forward to the next day when she would meet her work of art.

Adam had decided that fish really wasn't going to cut it. He was starting to regret his decision not to eat Princess Clarice because she was looking tastier by the minute. When another one of her lackeys showed up – this one with a tail – he shifted his attention. Maybe he could just eat one of them? They were built wrong anyway. He might just do everyone a favour and start on them. They wouldn't be missed, would they?

Princess Clarice started to get bored – the conversation hadn't really continued after the smell comment – so she excused herself and headed for the ladies' room. Of course this left Adam completely free and able to execute his plan. The next man with a construction fault was going to be in trouble.

That's when beak-man entered the room to clear the table.

Adam hastily sprang to his feet, still feeling a bit famished – soup and fish really weren't as filling as people – and hurried over to the startled man. Shep, who had been waiting for something like this to happen, immediately jumped out from under the table and gave his best 'Are you freaking kidding me?' barks. Unfortunately this did not deter Adam, who had already smacked the unsuspecting man on the head with the empty platter. He had just stuffed the man's hand – still attached to his arm – in his mouth, when he heard the most awful sound in the world. He dropped the hand and turned to the door, where Princess Clarice

121

was screaming her head off. This was not going quite as planned.

Princess Clarice's face was starting to turn bright red, and Adam could hear heavy footsteps coming quickly down the hallway. Shep pulled his sleeve, while also trying to back away from the unconscious man with his slightly bloody hand. He really had an awful taste in masters, but what could he do about it now? Try and save his current one, for sure.

The thundering footsteps kept getting closer and closer. Adam suddenly jumped up and asked Shep, "Now what?"

Shep just barked once and sprinted through the open concealed door and hoped that Adam was smart enough to follow him. He was. Together they stumbled into the kitchen. Shep sniffed and could smell the cool night air: they were close to an open door. He spotted it on the other side of the kitchen and ran for his life with Adam in his wake.

They could still hear yelling inside – had Princess Clarice taken a breath yet, or had her face turned purple by now? Not really wanting to find out, they ran headlong into the night. Fortunately the first guard they had met was the distracted kind and had forgotten to lock the outside gate. They burst through it and set off to the right, running as fast as their legs could carry them.

When they got to the bridge they had rested under before, Shep motioned to Adam to go down the embankment. Adam, who was very happy to take a breather, quickly slipped down the slope. He didn't know what to do, but he was certain that Shep would come up with an amazing plan. Both of them sat down under the bridge and assumed a thinking pose.

*

Petulia had had enough. She had become closely acquainted with several books and magazines while Gabriel and Miss Level had been inside the tent. She couldn't wait any longer and strode over to the tent. When she opened the flap and stuck her head through, she saw them hastily stepping away from each other.

"Oh, forget it. I know what's going on. You don't have to hide it any more. I can only hope that this tent is a lot more book-proof than it is soundproof."

She walked in and closed the zipper behind her. After that, she just sort of collapsed on the floor and waited. It didn't take too long for a book to smash into the roof of the tent. Petulia, Miss Level and Gabriel only heard a small thud. Thanks to the dome-shaped roof, the book slid gently down the side and fell to the floor. The roof itself stayed firm. Petulia closed her eyes and smiled.

"At least you did something right."

Miss Level stepped a bit closer. "Look, I'm sorry." Gabriel stepped up next to her. "We're sorry. We didn't mean for this to happen. It just…kind of did. I'm not even sure what happened… but I know I like it, I mean him, well, Gabriel…"

"Oh, shut up. We'll figure it out tomorrow. Now I just want to go to sleep. Do you have any idea how tiring it can be to be smacked in the head constantly?" Petulia rolled her head sideways to look at Miss Level, who was holding hands with Gabriel. "I don't suppose you do." With those words she turned on her other side and settled down to sleep. It didn't take too long before her snores resounded throughout the tent.

Miss Level and Gabriel looked at each other, smiled and lay down to go to sleep as well. Miss Level waved her hand over both of them, creating a blanket from the grass.

Chief Hightower was pacing across the dining room of the palace. A red-faced Princess Clarice was sitting at the head of the table with a man with a tail next to her, fanning her with a dented serving tray. At least she had stopped screaming.

Chief Hightower looked to the other side of the table, where a man with a beak was being looked after by a doctor. The doctor was currently wrapping gauze around his injured hand. Inspector Small walked up to him, followed by an officer from the special crimes unit. It was the same techie who had examined the scene in The Last Call.

"Jones has something for you, Chief."

"Yes?" The chief looked at him expectantly.

"Well, I must say it's quite extraordinary." Jones rummaged through his bag and drew out two moulds. He handed the first one to the chief. "This was taken from the remains of the leg we found at The Last Call."

The chief took the mould. "What am I looking at here?"

"These are teeth marks, left by the assailant, when he was chewing on the leg."

"Okay." The chief took a closer look, not quite sure why he was looking at a piece of evidence from a different crime scene.

"And these were taken, just now, from that man's hand." Jones pushed the second mould into the chief's hands.

Chief Hightower looked from the first mould to the second,

then made a close comparison of both. "These are the same." He looked up at Jones, who was smiling brightly.

"That they are."

"Which means we can put a face to our killer."

"That we can."

The chief turned to look at Princess Clarice. "Well, we can once she has stopped sobbing and can give us a concrete description."

The three of them now stared at Princess Clarice and the fanning tail-man. Three sighs resounded in the dining room. The chief resumed his pacing, while Inspector Small and Jones sat down in two vacant chairs.

They had been sitting under the bridge for several hours. Shep knew that they had to get out of the city as quickly as possible. He had noticed an old gate on their way to the bridge and figured this was their best chance of escape. He pulled Adam's sleeve to get him to start moving. Reluctantly Adam got up and followed Shep back up the slope. Both of them ran stealthily across the street, sticking close to the buildings.

When they finally got to the gate, Shep yanked the cord with his teeth and waited impatiently for the guard to open it. A lot of clinking and clanking later, the gate opened up and a smiling young man appeared.

"My, I am lucky. This is the second time in twenty-four hours that I've opened this gate. Had my father still been alive, he'd be green with envy." He cocked his head, looking at the man and dog standing in front of him. "But isn't it a bit early for this? The sun is barely coming up."

They didn't have time for this. Shep ran past the man, hoping Adam would follow. Adam was surprised to see Shep take off so quickly, but wasted no time hesitating. He pushed the man aside and ran after his dog.

The man fell to the ground and watched the duo sprint away. "How rude."

Just as they rounded the corner, all of the bells in the city started to chime. They were loud, and very alarming. The man, still sitting on the ground, looked back at the gate, and then to where the duo had disappeared.

"This can't be good."

Eleven

Heaven Knows

Petulia opened one of her eyes, just a crack. She didn't like bells in general but now they were just exaggerating. Really…

Miss Level and Gabriel were also woken by the bells. "What's going on?"

"Does it look like I know what's going on?" Petulia raised one eyebrow while asking this question. "Why don't the two of you go outside and check it out? I'll stay here where I won't get hit by any passing books."

Miss Level shrugged and motioned for Gabriel to follow her. When Petulia was moody – and let's face it, when was she ever not moody? – there was nothing else to do but to stay out of her way.

She opened the zipper and stepped out of the tent. The tent really wasn't soundproof at all – bloody bells sounded just as loud out here. She walked around the tent with Gabriel right behind her and looked in the general direction of Clariceville. They didn't really notice anything wrong.

Suddenly it seemed like there was an echo of the bells. Miss

Level and Gabriel turned around simultaneously and frowned – also simultaneously.

"That's Heaven." Miss Level was stunned. "What's wrong in Heaven?"

A black plume of smoke rose above the treeline – they couldn't actually see the city itself. The smoke kept billowing up. Suddenly there was an explosion so big that a wave of warm air hit them.

Inside the tent, Petulia had felt the shock wave of the explosion as well. Curiosity got the better of her – and she was wide awake now anyway – so she got up and mentally prepared herself for the onslaught of books she was going to face in order to find out what had happened. She opened the zipper and immediately noticed the thick black smoke rising up from behind the trees. Gabriel and Miss Level were standing next to the tent, staring dumbfounded in the same direction.

"What happened?" Petulia joined them.

"I don't know." Miss Level couldn't stop staring in the direction of Heaven City. There really was a lot of smoke. This wasn't just one house that had caught fire – this was the entire city. The bells of Heaven City were still going but the sound was being drowned out by the collapsing buildings.

Miss Level tried to make sense of this, but couldn't. "This is big. Should we go over there and find out if we can help?"

At this point the three of them saw a small, flying ball of fire coming their way. Not sure what to make of this, they just followed it with their eyes.

"Damn it." Petulia quickly turned and ran into the tent just in time. The small ball of fire turned out to be a magic book, heading straight for her. Fortunately it collided with the side of the tent before it could do any damage to Petulia's head.

"It might not be soundproof but it sure is fireproof." Miss Level walked over to the book that was thrashing around on the floor. She stepped on it a few times to put out the fire. Then she carefully picked it up. "What book is this?"

The lettering was completely charred off the cover. Slowly Miss Level opened the book, trying hard not to damage it any further. Her eyes opened wide when she figured out the tiny words on the first page.

"Petulia – you'll never guess what's happened!" Miss Level grabbed the still-moving book and entered the tent. Before she could do anything, the book flew out of her hands and straight into Petulia's head. Then it stopped and fell hard to the floor.

"Damn it. Are you crazy? Do you want me to get decapitated by murderous books?"

Miss Level was too excited to be insulted. "Look at it."

Reluctantly, Petulia ducked and lifted the book. "It's burned." She turned it around. "Doesn't make it hurt any less on impact, though," she mumbled. When she opened the book and focused on the tiny letters, all other criticisms dried up on her lips. "Is this what I think it is?"

Miss Level nodded vigorously, smiling brightly.

Petulia frowned. "Moss green? Really? Couldn't you have picked another colour?" She dropped the book onto the floor. "Well, do your thing. Change it back. Just wait until I'm outside. I don't want to get hit by another wayward spell." And with those words she charged out of the tent.

Miss Level crossed to the middle of the tent and carefully arranged the tiny *Big Book of Dale* in front of her. She stayed still for a few moments, clearing her head to focus on the spell. When she began chanting a few words, she started to give off the purple glow again. Her hand hovered over the book. The book started to quake. It grew in every direction and became its own bright red colour again, char-free. When it dropped back to the floor, it seemed to give a sigh of relief. Miss Level opened her eyes, happy to see the right result.

She picked up the book, walked out of the tent and handed it to Petulia. "There you go. I also fixed the location spell so you shouldn't get hit in the head by any other books." She smiled and turned to Gabriel.

"Well, good." The cleverest retort Petulia could come up with at that time. She figured it didn't matter anyway.

Adam and Shep had been running for a while when they came across a tiny, crooked farmhouse. Shep noticed that Adam was having trouble following him, so he barked once and jumped over the tiny fence surrounding it. Adam wasn't really sure what Shep was planning but figured he should probably just follow him. He just hoped the running would stop for a while. He opened the gate in the fence and walked into the garden. It was well tended and Adam immediately felt at ease. He was gazing around when Shep suddenly grabbed his sleeve and pulled him down to the ground.

"What is it?" Adam looked around cautiously. The bells were still ringing and he was fairly certain they might have something to do with him. Although he wasn't sure what it all meant, he had decided to follow Shep, who seemed to know what he was doing.

All of a sudden a small, stocky dwarf appeared, carrying a pitchfork. "What are you doing here?" He was waving his pitchfork around dangerously. "Well?"

"Euhm…"

Shep noticed a sign and barked. Adam looked at him, and then in the direction Shep was nodding to.

"We would like some vegetables."

The dwarf squeezed his eyes into suspicious slits. "Then why are you sitting in our rose bushes?"

"Inspecting them from up close. They are very nice. Can we see the vegetable patches as well?" Somehow Adam managed to improvise.

The dwarf seemed to consider it, and was about to tell them to shove off when the female dwarf appeared. "New customers?" She smiled brightly.

Before the male dwarf could say anything, the female had already invited them in. Adam and Shep didn't hesitate – better to be inside somewhere than out in the open.

The sound of hoof beats came closer and closer. Petulia, who was still staring at *The Big Book of Dale* in her hands, didn't notice them at first. But when Miss Level and Gabriel started to walk towards the road, she glanced up and decided to join them.

When they reached the road, they could see a cloud of dust approaching from Heaven. Not being able to control their curiosity, they just watched it come closer. Finally they could see a horse-drawn carriage in the middle of the cloud. It was rushing towards them.

When it reached them, the driver immediately stopped the carriage. The four horses were very glad of this and almost collapsed in exhaustion.

The door of the carriage opened and a very angry God appeared. "Why aren't you at home? I need more time to figure out what to say to you."

"Well, that's just too bad because here we are. You might as well come out with it." Petulia glowered at him. She had never liked God, and now that she had seen how he treated his horses, her dislike only grew.

God noticed *The Big Book of Dale* in Petulia's arms – seeing that it was back to its usual size and colour, it would have been hard not to notice it. The presence of the book only seemed to anger him further.

"I see you have gotten your book back." His eyes squeezed into fine slits. "You did this on purpose, didn't you?" His index finger was very close to poking Petulia's arm.

At this, Petulia's right eyebrow rose and she said, "If you want to lose that finger, I can tell you, you're on the right track."

"Don't be haughty with me. You have no right!" But God did lower his finger.

"Oh, really? And why is that?"

"You sent that book to me!" Unconsciously, he pointed to *The Big Book of Dale.* "It was disguised very well but you knew I would know what it was." God's anger only seemed to grow bigger and bigger.

Miss Level instinctively knew that she had better take over this conversation. No matter what Petulia might say now, it could only have disastrous results.

Just as Petulia opened her mouth, Miss Level said, "We would never do something like that. What good would it do?"

God slowly turned to face Miss Level. "Because you knew I have wanted this book since the first time I heard about it."

Before she could help it, she put her hands on her waist in pure Petulia fashion and replied, "Then you should have just looked harder. It's our book and we are not letting it go."

God also put his hands on his waist. "Then why was it disguised and flying through my city?"

They immediately fell into a staring contest. Petulia looked at them, noticing the postures they had adopted, and wondered if she looked just as silly whenever she did this. She shook her head, made a mental note to try and avoid striking that pose again, and waved her hand between them.

"Look. We didn't send you *The Big Book of Dale* on purpose and we are sorry for any inconvenience it has caused." She tried to smile, but had been out of practice for so long that it looked very false.

A bit unsettled by the smile, Miss Level stammered, "Yes, uhm, yes. We're, uhm, sorry." She directed her attention back to God to keep from seeing that smile any longer – it was going to haunt her for all time.

"Inconvenience? Of course it was an inconvenience! Can you not see my city burning?" Now God started pointing at the black plume of smoke.

"Well, yes." Miss Level looked from the smoke to God. "But how did the book cause this? It's just a book." She frowned at him.

"Just a book? It's the greatest book of all, as I mentioned in my predictions. Remember?" He looked longingly at *The Big Book of Dale*, still in Petulia's arms. "I couldn't let it go, could I? I had to try and turn it back." The anger that had been God's companion since he left the burning city of Heaven faded and was replaced by shame, sorrow and longing.

It was quiet for a while until Miss Level finally realised what this meant. Very quietly, she asked, "So it was you who destroyed Heaven?"

The shame completely drowned out all other emotions. God buried his face in his hands and dropped to the floor.

"I don't understand how this could have happened." Soft sobs drifted up from where he was sitting.

Petulia, Miss Level and Gabriel looked at each other, not quite knowing what to do. Fortunately at that exact moment they heard new hoof beats. This time they were coming from Clariceville.

The male dwarf was standing at the window, looking out.

"What is it?" The female's smile had faded the tiniest bit since they had heard the horseman passing on the road.

"City guard." The male chanced a glance at the female. "Just one, though. Don't they usually ride out in pairs?"

Shep noticed the smile on the female's face waver a bit more, right before a completely insincere one took over – it didn't reach her eyes any more. Shep was well aware that the lone guard was probably looking for his master. But as long as the dwarves didn't kick them out, they would be all right.

The male dwarf stretched his arms over his head and yawned. "Dear me, look at the time. Shouldn't you two be off?"

Before Adam could point out it was barely morning, the female joined in and practically pushed them out the door, mumbling something about staying up all night and needing to get some sleep. Not five minutes later Shep and Adam were staring, dumbfounded, at the closing door.

"How rude."

Shep barked once and then pulled Adam's sleeve to get him moving – it was becoming such a habit that the fabric was starting to tear.

Inside the house the male dwarf headed towards the bathroom with a basket full of mushrooms. "We can't take any chances."

Twelve

Let's Wrap it Up

A lone horseman pulled up to Petulia, Miss Level, Gabriel and God. He had noticed the black smoke coming from Heaven.

"What happened?" he asked, bewildered, staring at the smoke.

This, of course, only made God sob harder.

"It was an accident." Petulia waved her hand in a dismissive way.

"But…but…I was sent to Heaven for help," the city guard stammered.

"Well, they could probably use a hand." Petulia frowned at the man, not quite sure why he was still there, talking to them.

"No, *we* need *their* help."

This made Petulia frown harder. "Who are 'we'?" She shook her head. "Never mind. I don't want to know. It looks like you're going to have to find someone else anyway."

The horseman slid down from his horse and sat next to God in the exact same position – head in hands. "This won't do. It just won't."

Petulia, Miss Level and Gabriel looked at each other and then back at the two sobbing figures at their feet.

"No, it won't," Petulia muttered.

Chief Hightower gazed intently into the eyes of the man sitting in front of him at the table in the palace.

"Are you sure?"

The man nodded vigorously. "Yes, positive. That's the man who left the city this morning. I opened the gate myself."

When Princess Clarice had finally snapped out of it earlier that morning, the city guard sketch artist had been able to do his thing. The drawing of the suspect looked like an ordinary man, albeit a very handsome one.

The chief was still sceptical. "You must see a hundred people a day walk through that gate."

The man started to blush. "To be honest, it was only the second time I opened the gate. But twice in one day – I felt lucky. Now I'm not so sure." The man looked at the chief and clearly saw the disbelief in his eyes. "The South Gate is much more popular. Just ask Gerald." Mumbling, "Even though mine does have a direct road to Heaven."

Thanks to his excellent hearing Chief Hightower understood the man perfectly and was immediately annoyed that he hadn't thought of this himself. Of course the cannibal left through that gate: he was en route to his next hunting ground. The chief sprang up, startling the gatekeeper, and practically ran outside. To his surprise, he ran straight into Inspector Small, who had come in to warn him.

"Chief, there are some people here to see you."

"Not now." He had only just muttered those words when he noticed the rather large crowd forming in front of the palace.

"I'm afraid you don't really have a choice." Inspector Small stood next to the chief, both of them looking outside.

The chief sighed. He should have seen this one coming as well. Maybe he was losing his touch. "Angry mob?"

"Yup."

"Torches?"

"Uh-huh."

"Pitchforks?"

"Counted thirty-eight."

The chief sighed again. There wasn't a lot you could do about an angry mob, hell-bent on blood. "Let's go and talk to them."

As they started to move towards the door, the inspector quietly mentioned, "I'm pretty sure they are beyond the point of reason but we'll see how it goes."

The chief hated this part of the job, but he straightened his back anyway and faced the crowd.

Still a little confused by the sudden eviction from the dwarves' house, Shep and Adam walked down the road, away from Clariceville.

Shep figured that, as long as the city guard was ahead of them, it didn't matter how fast they walked. To any outsider they just looked like a man walking his dog. Nothing wrong with that.

Petulia turned away from the sobbing men. She opened *The Big Book of Dale* and quickly conjured up a massive cauldron.

"Gabriel?" She glanced over her shoulder. "Would you mind looking around for some firewood?"

He smiled in response, gently kissed the back of Miss Level's hand and off he went.

Miss Level gazed longingly after him for a moment and then joined her friend. "What are you doing?"

"To be honest I'm just really hungry. I'm going to make soup."

"Sounds wonderful." Miss Level turned back to God and the horseman and said, "If you two don't stop moping, there will be no soup for you."

Both men looked up like two petulant boys.

In response, Miss Level assumed a Petulia pose and raised her right eyebrow. "Well?"

They crossed their arms in unison, and muttered, also in unison, "Fine."

"That's what I thought. Come on, get up. You're helping us clean the vegetables."

Reluctantly they rose and followed Miss Level to the cauldron. At the same time, Gabriel came back with his arms full of twigs and branches.

"Why don't you just use magic? I hardly ever do manual labour any more." God held up a carrot as if it was crawling with tiny bugs. He scowled at it.

"Perhaps that's why you blew up Heaven," Petulia replied.

God pretended not to hear, grabbed the carrot more firmly

and started scraping the damned thing. Miss Level pretended not to hear it too and quietly sent a tiny purple flame to the stack of twigs, which promptly caught fire.

Chief Hightower had actually managed to calm the people down. Unfortunately, that's when the gatekeeper decided to leave. As soon as he stepped through the door, one rather clever man exclaimed that he was the gatekeeper of the West Gate.

"So why is he here, then? Did the man leave the city? Did he go through his gate? Is he going to Heaven?" The questions kept coming and the chief wasn't fast enough to answer all of them. The crowd took this as confirmation and immediately set off for the West Gate.

"Oh my, I'd better go and open it." The gatekeeper rushed off before the chief could stop him.

"Inspector Small, I feel that this case might be my last one. I'm clearly losing my touch. Perhaps it is time to step down."

Not quite knowing what to say or do, the inspector just replied, "A man's got to do what a man's got to do."

It wasn't quite the reply the chief had expected. A bit of pleading would have been nice. But he supposed it wasn't in the inspector's nature. Perhaps he should stay a little while longer, just to explain these kinds of things to him. The chief and the inspector joined the other city guards, climbed on their horses and followed the angry mob.

All of a sudden Shep started to feel very uncomfortable. He looked around for a clue as to what had alerted his doggy senses. Adam, who was oblivious to his unease, just kept walking with his hands in his pockets. They were rounding a corner when Shep suddenly yanked on Adam's sleeve, causing both of them to tumble into a small ditch.

"What the…?" Adam tried to stand up to brush the dirt from his clothes, but Shep wouldn't let go. Finally realising how tenacious Shep was being, he hunkered down next to him. "What is it?"

With a soft whining noise Shep motioned to the clearing they had been about to embark upon. Adam peered over the side of the ditch and between a few trees. He could see two weird-looking women and three men standing around a huge cauldron.

One of the men was doing something funny with a carrot while the other two were scraping potatoes. The oldest-looking woman was stirring a ladle in the pot and the other one was on her haunches, checking out the flames. He couldn't quite explain it but this image made him feel complete somehow.

Shep, on the other hand, knew perfectly well that these people were witches. Why else would they be standing around a gigantic cauldron? He hadn't known that there was such a thing as a male witch, though. And to find three of them right here – what were the odds?

Miss Level was sitting on her haunches, staring hard at the side of the cauldron. She was certain that someone was watching them, so she tried to look around inconspicuously, using the reflection in the cauldron's surface. Couldn't Petulia have conjured up a shiny new one? It was really hard trying to see anything in this bloody old thing.

Wait a minute. Was that movement between those trees? She squinted even harder but could see nothing.

"What are you doing?" Petulia looked down. "The fire is good. You should help the amateur cooks over there, before all of the water has boiled away."

"I just have this feeling…" Miss Level's sentence faded away.

Petulia rolled her eyes. "Yes, I know about your feelings. Well, I'm feeling hungry, damn it. So start scraping or peeling something."

Reluctantly Miss Level got up and grabbed a carrot.

What was that noise? Shep could hear a vague rumbling from behind them. He turned around and peeked over the side of the ditch.

His eyes widened in shock. A crowd of people were steadily marching towards them, waving pitchforks and torches. He quickly looked around for any kind of escape route, but found none. Talk about being stuck between a rock and a hard place: witches or angry mob, which would it be?

He glanced at Adam, who was still mesmerised by the people around the cauldron. At least the witches looked rather friendly, and Adam seemed to like them. Shep decided they would just have to do and nudged Adam with his nose.

"What is it?" Adam gently put his hand on Shep's head and stroked it.

Somewhat comforted by the gesture, Shep nudged him again and climbed out of the ditch, between the two trees. Adam smiled and followed.

*

The hair on the back of Miss Level's neck stood up. She shivered and turned sideways to Gabriel. He had gone completely white and was standing stock-still at the edge of the cauldron. She gently put her hand on his lower back for comfort. The gesture thawed him and his shoulders sank a bit. Slowly Miss Level turned further around and saw a man and a dog coming towards them. She instinctively knew it had been them watching from between the trees. She could feel it.

She could also feel that there was something off about the man. The closer he came, the more certain she was. Although he appeared ordinary, there was a vague outline surrounding him; a kind of dark aura that seemed to grow with every step he took. Miss Level felt a tingle in her hand and realised it was still resting on Gabriel's back. When she looked at it, she noticed Gabriel too had an aura surrounding him. This one was silvery, almost like a mist that clung to him.

Gabriel turned towards Miss Level and gave her a sad little smile. He could feel that his time was running out quickly. He didn't know how he had come into this world, just that Miss Level and Petulia had something to do with it. He didn't understand a lot of the world either, but he was glad to have been part of it. But now it felt like he had to say goodbye. He could feel a strange pull towards the man walking across the field, and there was nothing he could do about it.

Miss Level gazed into Gabriel's eyes and instinctively knew what it was about the stranger with the dog that made her feel uncomfortable, yet somehow felt familiar. She needed a moment to process everything, to decide what to do, but she didn't have a moment.

"What's happening?" Petulia, who had been oblivious to everything that was going on, heard a rumbling noise. She looked up from her cauldron, which still had only water in it.

She noticed the man with the dog, quickly decided the noise wasn't coming from them – but didn't that man look familiar? – and gazed down the road towards Clariceville. God and the horseman followed her example. All three of them were rather surprised to see an angry mob rounding the corner, but when the man and dog hesitated and eventually stopped walking, the three shifted their attention towards the strange duo.

The horseman slowly reached behind him and pulled out a piece of paper. He unfolded it and glanced from the paper to the man and back again. He did this several times before it dawned on him that it really was the same man. He immediately dropped the paper, grabbed a stick lying nearby and shouted for the man to hold it right there.

This caused the following sequence of events to happen:

The leader of the angry mob turned towards them and quickly deduced that this was the man they were after. Why else would a city guard yell at a man walking his dog?

Captain Hightower and Inspector Small spurred their horses on so they could beat the crowd to the scene.

Petulia frowned and asked what the hell was going on, damn it.

God lifted his carrot in defence, alarmed by the sudden seriousness of the horseman.

Gabriel winced.

And Miss Level closed her eyes and froze time and space. Accidentally. She just needed a bit more time.

Thirteen

The Beginning of the End

When Miss Level opened her eyes and saw the tableau of frozen people and animals in front of her, she startled. Had she done that? How?

She turned towards the frowning Petulia. Frozen solid. It was not a good look for her. A little further away, God with his carrot and the horseman with his stick looked like they were fighting each other. The mob and the two men on horseback were too far off to notice anything in particular about them. But the man and the dog, now there was a mystery.

Miss Level quietly tiptoed around the cauldron – quite pointless, because none of the others could hear her anyway. She made her way to the strange duo and scrutinised them. The dark aura still surrounded the man. When Miss Level put her hand out to touch the black mist, she felt an electric current run through her veins. The moment her finger entered the mist-like substance, a tiny purple lightning bolt escaped her fingertip and hit the man's upper left arm. Miss Level cocked her head, but could see no other effect. She withdrew her hand and stepped back.

A loud moaning came from behind her. When Miss Level turned back in surprise, she could see God moving his head. Then slowly his shoulders, then his arms, until his entire body was freed.

"How did you...?"

"It doesn't matter." God scowled. "How did *you*?"

"I don't know. I just needed some time."

God looked around. "Well, you got it." He walked towards Miss Level and the frozen stranger. "What do we have here?" He scrutinised the man just as effectively as Miss Level had done a few moments before.

"Can you see it?"

"See what?" God stood nose to nose with the stranger.

From Miss Level's point of view, his nose was completely swallowed up by the black mist.

"The blurry black outline. You can't see it, can you?"

"Blurry black outline, eh?" He perused the man. "Nope. Must be your imagination."

Miss Level squinted at him. "How did you unfreeze?"

He waved his hand dismissively in her direction. "I cast a spell on myself ages ago to avoid being frozen by anyone. Mostly because of my ex. I don't quite understand how you were able to freeze me, though." He lifted his right hand and rubbed his bearded chin pensively.

Empowered by this news, Miss Level stepped closer. "Well, don't think I won't do it again. Now get out of my way!"

God was thrown aside by some unseen force and ended up unconscious between the trees.

"Huh." It was all Miss Level could think of to say. She stared at the crumpled heap of God in the distance. "Well."

After a minute or two – when she was certain that God wasn't coming back with a vengeance – she turned back to the man with the dog. Why could she see the black aura but God couldn't? She was fairly certain that Petulia hadn't noticed it either. Well, before she got frozen anyway.

Miss Level suddenly remembered that Gabriel had a similar outline, but his was silvery. It had only appeared when this man came out from between the trees. Which meant that the two men were linked. Which meant that this man was the 'something' they had forgotten in the theatre. Well then, she just had to fix this.

She stepped back until she was right in the middle between Gabriel and the stranger. Then she closed her eyes and concentrated. The grass tent, standing a little further away, started to crumble. Where the grass fell down in a heap, purple dust twirled up into the air. The fire under the cauldron died down. As it did, purple smoke rose up.

Some of the frozen people began to twitch a little, coming back to life. Purple tendrils seemed to escape them. The dust, smoke and tendrils moved towards each other and eventually blended together, right above Miss Level. She was calling back all the magic she had used for these things, knowing she would need every ounce of it.

More and more people became aware of their surroundings again and looked around in confusion. They didn't know what was going on but they had a general feeling that interrupting it would be a very bad idea.

Even Petulia was stumped by what she was seeing, but she decided to just wait it out. It was never a good idea to disrupt a spell, and this one looked like a whopper.

When Shep came to, he immediately started to bark, to try and warn Adam. But the sound was transformed into vibrating purple bubbles. They lifted up into the air and blended with the smoky purple cloud above the weird-looking woman. Quickly realising he was only helping the witch, Shep promptly shut his yap.

Using all the energy she could get, Miss Level focused her spell and started binding the different energies together. The dust clung to the tendrils and knitted together with the smoke. Gabriel and the strange man were the only two still left frozen. It took all Miss Level's concentration to keep them that way. Then, slowly, the silvery mist surrounding Gabriel lifted and joined the knot of energy above Miss Level's head. This made the knot shine brightly, giving off a violet hue.

The surrounding people protected their eyes with their hands but could not help trying to see what would happen next. They didn't have to wait too long. The shiny knot drifted closer to the stranger until it was right above him. It tumbled over and over, as if in anticipation of something.

From somewhere deep within Miss Level's pocket a tiny amount of ash rose up and landed smack in the middle of the knot, making a mark and causing it to stop tumbling. The dark aura surrounding the man also rose up, and hit the mark.

The knot shook and vibrated. Then it stretched out and a crack formed within it. Tiny at first, but the more the knot stretched, the more the crack grew until it was a fissure in the sky, with nothing but darkness inside it. The edges of the unravelled knot bent down and grabbed the stranger, like tiny arms and hands grappling for something to hold on to. Unable to stop them, the stranger was soon covered in curling, purplish branches, pulling him up.

The dog snapped at the branches to no avail. There were too many of them, growing too quickly. He could only watch, like the rest of the people, as the man was pulled up and swallowed by the darkness in the fissure.

Then, with a snap, the fissure closed and Miss Level promptly fainted.

Chief Hightower had watched the entire thing from the moment he became unfrozen. He was amazed and awed, and a little unsure of what to do next. He looked around and noticed he wasn't the only one. The people surrounding him were staring at the purple cloud and the fainted woman. Then the murmurs started. The murmurs became ramblings. And the ramblings turned into shouting.

Chief Hightower motioned to Inspector Small, who promptly came over.

"We should get the people back to the city."

"Yup."

"Any ideas?"

"Nope."

"Well, you're no help at all."

Chief Hightower turned away and rode his horse to the front of the mob. Maybe he could just ask them nicely to go home.

*

Gabriel knelt, with Miss Level's head in his lap. He had woken up from his frozen state at the exact moment when she collapsed. Unsure of what had happened, he had raced towards her and lifted her gently into his arms.

Petulia could not believe the power Miss Level possessed. She had always tried to calm her when the purple glow appeared, but now she knew better. It was Miss Level's power manifesting. And it was huge. She was a full-blown, natural witch. No more spells going awry, no more haggling for commissions. Now if only she would wake up…

With Petulia pacing next to him, Gabriel gently rubbed Miss Level's arms in an attempt to rub some life back into her. It took about fifteen minutes but finally Miss Level's eyes opened.

"Did it work?" She gazed up into Gabriel's eyes, happy that he was still there.

"Did it work?" Petulia bent down. "You didn't even know if it would work? What were you thinking? You know very well that you can't just go around casting spells without the proper knowledge or experience." When she realised she was scolding a very powerful witch, she promptly shut her mouth and turned around to fetch the cauldron.

Gabriel felt like he should say something. Unfortunately the only effect the spell had had on him was lifting the aura. So when he opened his mouth, this is what he said.

"*I think that you're amazing, and I thank God you're not dead. I can't help all this praising, of the loveliest woman I've ever met.*"

"You shouldn't thank God. He had nothing to do with it." But Miss Level smiled and kissed him anyway.

That's actually about the time God reappeared, rubbing his head vigorously. He stumbled across the field towards Petulia.

"So you decided to join us again, eh?" Petulia tipped the cauldron out, pretty sure there wasn't going to be any soup anyway. "Couldn't stand the heat, eh?"

"I'm not really sure what happened. One moment I was standing next to Miss Level and the next moment I woke up next to a tree."

He seemed completely bewildered, so Petulia decided to stop giving him a hard time.

"Really?"

"Yes." Still rubbing his head. "I'm pretty sure it had something to do with Miss Level. She was shouting at me."

Petulia glanced over to her friend and inwardly thanked her. God occasionally needed to be put in his place and she was glad Miss Level had done so.

She turned back to God. "Well, why don't you think it over on your way home?"

God nodded absently and walked towards Heaven City, which was still smouldering a bit but it would be all right.

"Shouldn't we tell him?" Miss Level got up and stood next to Petulia, watching God walk away.

"Tell him what? That he has won?" Petulia shrugged. "He was here. He'll figure it out soon enough and come knocking on our door, wagging his finger and doing his stupid little 'I told you so' dance. Personally, I can go a few days longer without seeing that." She glanced sideways to Miss Level. "Can't you?"

"Well, if you put it that way…" Miss Level turned around, lifted her bag and motioned for Gabriel to follow them home.

To his amazement, asking nicely had actually worked. Chief Hightower watched the last of the citizens walk back to Clariceville. He looked around and noticed a scruffy-looking dog by the side of the road. He looked lost. Maybe one of the Claricevilleans had forgotten him.

It had been a rather strange experience to be here, watching that woman do her thing. He actually felt a bit used somehow. So it was only natural to forget things. The chief looked back at the dog. It shouldn't be too hard to figure out whom he belonged to, so he waved at the dog to come closer.

Shep cocked his head and stared at the man on the horse. He wasn't so fond of horses, but the man looked all right. He couldn't do any worse than his last two masters. Crap, there was that word again. He dropped his head slightly and trotted behind the man on the horse, all the while pondering the reasons for loyalty towards masters.